SEDUCTION

SEDUCTION

SEDUCTION

a novel

Emily Martin

atmosphere press

I

He was of average height, but everything about him was far from average. He was strikingly handsome in a Mediterranean way, with short, dark, lush hair, smooth olive skin, and dark hazel brown eyes with stubble lining his chiselled jaw. His arms were large and muscular. I imagined myself wrapped in them, safe and secure. I never could resist him, right from the first moment I tried, and in that instant, it felt like two bodies had, in essence, become one. It felt natural, and it felt like home.

It wasn't so much what he did to me that was extraordinary, but the way he made me feel— as if he had unearthed my soul and made me understand myself. I couldn't get my head around it; I'd had plenty of lovers before him to know the difference between being physically turned on and feeling a real connection. He certainly did something to me that first night; something had been reborn inside of me, and life was never going to be the same again.

"Phew, just about made it," I sighed as I pulled up into the office car park with only three minutes to spare until I officially started work. I never was an early bird and arriving each morning to the dull grey, dreary 1970s office block was no inspiration for me to leave my warm and cosy bed. "Morning, Karen, morning, John," I muttered as I rushed into my office, embarrassed that I had only just made it in on time once again.

I reluctantly turned on my computer and hung my coat up, ready for the day to begin. I looked around at everyone, watching as they operated like clockwork, happily plodding along with their routine of each day. My mind could not rest; I could not concentrate on the boring monotony of typing reports and answering emails and telephone queries. What had happened over the weekend and who was this amazing man I had met?! How had he managed to completely and wholly seduce my body yet still leave me feeling like I needed more?

It had been an average night out with Felicity; we were in the local nightclub, which was grotty and overpriced, with damp walls and sticky carpets that were once a vibrant red but now black from all the drinks that had been spilt over the years. The stench of stale beer mixed with cloying air freshener permeated the air. Felicity was, as usual, cool as a cucumber, swigging from her bottle of Bud, giving me the look that said, "Let's get out of here, this is rubbish," when they walked past us and smiled. We giggled to each other as they came over and introduced themselves. Jack was more confident but looked younger and shorter. Steve was more rugged with a larger build but kept back quietly behind Jack. Jack asked if we wanted a drink—we agreed and chatted, getting to know them a bit better.

The night was drawing to a natural close and the two boys asked us back to theirs for a nightcap. We quickly agreed. As far as I was concerned it was only one night and nothing would ever come of it. In the taxi on the way home, it became clear who was paired off with whom and Felicity and I laughed with the boys. When we arrived at the house, I had started to sober up and tiredness was setting in. "Nothing will happen between Jack and I, I won't let it," I whispered to Felicity as we went upstairs, confident in my words.

I went into one room and Felicity went into the other. I eagerly climbed up into the large, comfy, unmade bed; it was late, and I just wanted to sleep. The room was plain and uninspiring, a typical bachelor bedroom with clothes strewn about and body spray cans littering the floor. Jack came over, slowly and gently starting to kiss my lips and running his hands through my hair, testing where my boundaries lay with him. Although I had promised myself I would do nothing more than sleep and chat, I could not resist, so I let him touch me. The kissing grew more urgent and passionate. It was clear that he wanted more from me and at that point, so did I. I pulled my body closer to his and ran my hand down his toned chest, feeling the warmth of his body and the softness of his skin, breathing in his aftershave, taking every inch of him in. I gasped out loud with utter delight when I eventually slid my hand into his boxers and felt his huge manhood. The kissing and rubbing of each other's bodies became even more intense, and I decided to reach for the condom as a sign I wanted more to happen. I needed to feel him inside me right there and then! He carefully slid it on his beautifully hard penis while I sat up, eager for him to enter me. Once he was inside me, I knew there was no turning back as our bodies magically intertwined and moved together like they were one. Hot and sticky with sweat dripping down us both, we came together. I had never experienced anything so natural before.

I looked down and saw that the condom had split. I gasped and pulled back, turning away, annoyed at myself for having given in to my urges. I had recently come off the contraceptive pill and did not feel worried, but who knew where he had been before me!

His hand tenderly clasped my shoulder, and he asked if I was OK, his body spooning my bare back. I wasn't OK, for I knew I had given him a piece of my soul that was never to return. I had to have this again; he had taken me places my heart and my body had never known existed.

2

Tap, tap on my office door. "Hi, Louise, I need to update your software. Will you be out at lunch so I can use your PC?" The office manager had stepped in, breaking my train of thought.

"Yes, I shall be going out to the gym around 1 p.m., so you're welcome to use it then," I replied, eager for them to leave me alone. The rest of the day passed by completely uninteresting, and I only put half an effort into my workout as my mind just could not rest.

The next day at work, my phone beeped. It was a text from him: "*Hey, how's you?*" My heart skipped a beat and a smile spread across my face. I immediately texted back, and we ended up exchanging messages for the rest of the day. I was on cloud nine; he was attentive and eager. He made me giggle, and I could not wait to see him again. We had already arranged to meet up the next evening. Felicity and I usually went out that night during the week, so I asked if I could invite her along and for him to bring his friend Steve again. It looked set to be a great evening and it was all I could think about.

Finally, the time arrived. I put on a casual pair of jeans with a silky green vest top and matching green high-heeled court shoes. The taxi picked me up and along the way stopped for Felicity. Once at the pub, we sat down and waited for the guys to turn up. I told her how excited I was and how much I liked Jack. Then, soon enough, they were there. They sat down opposite us, and we started chatting. The conversation was strained between the other two and I asked if they wanted to move on to the club next door.

"Sure, let's go," Jack said and downed the last of his drink before pushing himself to his feet, expecting us to follow.

Once in the club, we bumped into some mutual friends and happily chatted away. I found myself drinking more and more and enjoying the atmosphere. "I need to move my car. I don't want to get a parking ticket," Jack said, his eyes running over my body. "Come with me..." I grabbed his hand; he didn't need to say any more.

We walked arm in arm down to the multi-story car park and he showed me where he had parked his dark blue BMW, in the corner, away from the other cars. He directed me to the passenger's door and then placed his hand on my cheek, moving my hair away from my face and leaning in to kiss me. The kiss was slow and tender; he trailed his hand down my torso and onto my trousers. I looked around to see if anyone else was about, but it was dark and deserted. I could not wait, and I pointed toward the bonnet of the car.

He laughed and said, "OK."

I quickly pulled my trousers and knickers down and perched on the edge of the bonnet. He unzipped his trousers, already hard, and teased me with his fingers; I grabbed at his collar and pulled him in close, asking him to pleasure me further. He thrust himself inside me and I let out a gasp. We moved together urgently, and he came quickly. Giggling, we moved apart and tidied ourselves up. "We had better get back to the others," I urged. We got in the car and drove closer to the club, laughing as we would have to go back in as if nothing had happened.

3

Once back in the club, I found Felicity dancing with Sarah, a regular there and a dance enthusiast. She had short, shiny, black, straight bobbed hair and was always styled impeccably along with the most welcoming smile. "Over here," Felicity beckoned. I said to Jack that I would be back in a moment and went on to meet my friends. Jack walked off and found a group of his friends over by Steve. The music and drinks were flowing; I was having a great time with Felicity and Sarah.

"So, how's it going with Jack then? He looks comfortable over there!" Sarah pointed to a corner of the club where Jack was grinding up against another girl.

"Hmmm, I thought it was going great," I muttered.

"He looks like he's a right flirt," Sarah continued while my blood ran hot with annoyance. "He's young; you know he's only nineteen, don't you? Liam told me."

"What?" I replied. He had told me he was twenty-one! *Oh, please don't let this be true*, I thought to myself. I had never even kissed a boy younger than me—it had never felt right—and five years younger was shocking. "You are joking, he can't be?!" I insisted.

"No, he really is. Steve and Liam are our age, but Jack is younger."

"What?! I'm so insulted," I replied, needing to get out of the club, not wanting to watch how Jack was behaving in front of me. "I think I'm going to get out of here," I declared to the girls and stormed off in search of the nearest taxi. I'd had enough of boys messing with my feelings and feeling hurt by Jack's lying and obvious lack of care for me. Witnessing him flirting with other girls had infuriated me. I did not want to show him how I felt, so I had to leave.

The next day at work flew past; my boss had an urgent report that needed to go out and I worked through my lunch break to get it organised. Missing my gym session at lunch, I decided to go after work. I put my headphones on and charged up and down the treadmill, letting all my negative thoughts diminish. I felt better after working up a sweat and went home in a lighter mood.

That evening, I phoned Felicity to see how she was. "I'm not sure about him. He just doesn't seem that sincere. Something doesn't add up. Be careful is all I will say." Her words stung—I had already started to get feelings for Jack, and I didn't like it, but as she was my best friend I listened attentively.

After putting the phone down, I went into the kitchen to start making an omelette for myself when I heard the familiar beep of my phone. It was a text from Jack saying he was on a train with Steve and a group of friends heading into London to a nightclub. No question of how I was, or why I had not said goodbye. Hastily I replied, "*That's great, have fun.*" Infuriated by my feelings, I turned my phone off, not wanting any more interaction from anyone. I wondered how I could feel so insecure so early on, and why he had not asked me to stay at his place last night. The thoughts ran through my mind, so after my dinner I went up to bed to get an early night and try to forget about him.

A few days went by, and Jack and I exchanged text messages. Things seemed to be back on track and Jack invited me over on the day of New Year's Eve. The weather had turned colder with the nights getting darker and it was a long journey to his house, down twisty country roads, and I was nervous driving into the unknown. Although we had been messaging, I was intrigued as to how he would act after our last night out. I pulled up into a modern cul-de-sac and parked my car on the drive.

"Hi, babe." Jack smiled. He opened the door cheerily in grey jogging bottoms and a striped T-shirt. He said he had been dozing on the sofa watching a sitcom and asked me if I wanted a drink.

"Yes, please, a juice or water would be great," I replied. Jack looked alluring in a craggy sort of way. He had told me he was renting a room in the house that Steve lived in but that he was alone today. I walked over to the sofa and sat down whilst Jack poured two orange juices. He placed the glasses on the table to the side of me and turned the TV down, sitting next to me. We talked about the TV show and threw plot twists back and forth, making polite conversation, skirting around the issue of how we had left our last meeting.

Jack then leaned over and put his arm around me and ran his fingers through my hair. It was warm inside the house, and I nestled into his arms. I tried to focus on the TV show, but feeling his breath against my face while my head lay on his chest was enough to make me want him. He lifted my chin, kissed my lips softly, and took my hand to his lap. My heart was beating faster and faster, and I knew what would happen, but I could not resist.

I moved my hand inside his jogging bottoms and slowly reached down to stroke his magnificent penis. It was already hard. He suddenly got up, went into the kitchen, and grabbed a bowl. He opened the freezer, placing a handful of ice cubes in the bowl.

"What are they for?" I asked.

"Just relax," he told me, pushing my skirt up and knickers to one side, sliding the ice up and down my clit. It felt strangely erotic, the look of control on his face boring into my eyes while he pleasured me with the ice and his fingers.

I reached down to my bag, grabbing a condom. "Put this on," I urged whilst I undressed myself, strip teasing in front of him, showing off my black satin lingerie set. I smiled and pushed him back into his seat whilst I straddled and positioned him inside me. He lovingly cupped his hands around my cheeks and stared into my eyes whilst I rode up and down rhythmically on him until I quietly came. He was still hard, and I wanted to please him, so I pulled the condom off and placed him inside my mouth, teasing him until he squirted hot salty semen into my mouth. The look on his face when I came up was of pure satisfaction, and I loved it. I wanted to please him as often as I could, and nothing would stop me.

"Enjoy that, did we?" he teased.

"I loved it." I winked at him, throwing his T-shirt at his face.

We both got dressed and cuddled on the sofa, watching old movies, stopping occasionally for snacks.

"You know, I heard a rumour that you were not twenty-one at all..." I edged the conversation, eager to know the truth.

"Err, yeh, I'm nineteen. I know I shouldn't have lied, but there was no way you would be interested in me if I had told you the truth."

I was surprised Jack had been so open. He was right, of course; I was twenty-four and would not have entertained him had I known he was nineteen, but as I was already happy with him, I tried to push it to the back of my mind. Soon it was late, and we were both going out that evening, so I left to get ready back at mine. We were going to the same place and agreed to see each other.

The whole drive home, I felt like I was on cloud nine. Whenever I was with Jack, he made me feel magical. I knew he was into me but there was still that air of mystery keeping me on my toes. I both loved and hated it at the same time. I knew I was falling quickly for him and wanted to stop myself, but the lust kept drawing me back in. He had this knack for pushing my boundaries further and further, but I enjoyed it! He was subtle yet forceful. I was intrigued to see where this would go.

4

My neat little two-bedroom starter home was cold and dark, a stark contrast to the warmth I had felt at Jack's. *"Still on for the New Year's party tonight?"* I had texted Felicity, eager to get dressed up and go out. *"You bet,"* she immediately responded. I put the music on full blast and got undressed. I picked out a bright pink dress and white shoes to wear to the club and then got into the shower. As usual, once I was ready, I got in the taxi and picked Felicity up on the way. We were out later than expected so we went straight into the club, eager to start drinking.

"So, what have you been up to today?" Felicity asked me as she had been at work.

"Oh, you know, sleeping with Jack, eeek!" I laughed, waiting for her reaction.

"Oh, I don't know about him, you know, he seems very shifty. Also, nineteen is too young!"

I smiled, ignoring her comment, not wanting to speak badly of him when I was still getting to know him—or possibly not wanting to hear the truth, I couldn't quite work it out.

Felicity and I chatted and danced, unaware of anyone around us, dancing like fools to get a laugh from each other. The drinks were flowing, and we were having a great night.

"I need the loo," I quickly shouted to Felicity and off I went to the toilet. On the way there I saw Jack walk past me. I grabbed his arm and smiled. He smiled back and said he would be back in a minute. I was excited to see him again and had butterflies dancing in my tummy.

Later that night, I texted him to ask where he was and if he wanted to come back to mine. He didn't reply. I could not understand where he was coming from and what kind of games he was playing. My heart sank a little as I continued the night with Felicity, not mentioning my text to her. The countdown came, "5, 4, 3, 2, 1, Happy New Year!" everyone in the club screamed as I hugged Felicity.

"This year will be our year," I shouted to her, excited as to what it could bring us both. I scanned the club but couldn't see Jack anywhere. I was determined not to let it ruin my night and went and got Felicity and me another drink each.

The next morning, I woke with a sore head from all the alcohol, hoping to find a message from Jack—but nothing. My pride was wounded, and I decided to keep busy and distract myself from thoughts of him.

The following days rolled into one as I eagerly waited to hear from Jack. My period was extremely late, and I was terrified. I had to bite the bullet and finally do a test. I went out on my lunch break at work and bought the test at the local supermarket. I waited until bedtime to do it and unwrapped it nervously. I had drunk a huge amount of water that evening and sat down to pee. My mind raced with thoughts of what I would do if I was pregnant. Finally, three minutes was up. I looked down and could not believe what the stick was saying. I was pregnant! I felt sick. I had just assumed that I would still be protected having been on the pill for such a long time and had mostly used condoms with Jack. Thoughts began racing through my mind: what I was going to do, how I could have let myself get into this situation. I was filled with utter disappointment and fear.

I grabbed my phone and texted Jack immediately to tell him. I had no other option. "Hey Jack, hope you are OK? We seriously need to talk. I'm pregnant." Short and sweet, to the point, there was no mucking about this time. I was still angry at the way he had behaved on New Year's Eve. My phone rang immediately. "Hey," I whispered as I answered.

"Hey, are you sure?" Jack replied hastily.

Had the man no people skills? Did he just not care?

"Yes, I am sure. I've just taken the test now. I was late for my period, but I kept ignoring it, hoping I wasn't. We do need to talk this through." I heard a short, sharp intake of breath and couldn't work out if it was him or me. This was serious and I was distraught. I put the phone down, sobbing.

We agreed to meet in a pub local to me at 8 p.m. the next evening. I was excited to see Jack again, but was feeling nervous as to how he would act. I decided to get dressed up, hoping to bring that spark back to him and completely ignoring the real reason we were meeting. I chose the highest heels I had in my wardrobe and a pair of tight dark blue ripped jeans with a loose-fitting off-the-shoulder T-shirt. I put on bright red lipstick and straightened my hair. Satisfied with how I looked, I got into my car, ready to drive to meet him.

I pulled up in the car park and texted him to say I was there. My heart was pounding, I was so nervous. Jack replied that he was already in the pub, so I walked in on my own. He came over as soon as he saw me. "Hey, how are you? What would you like to drink?" He leaned over to give me a kiss on the cheek.

"I'm OK, how are you?" I replied. He ordered a coffee, and I had an orange juice.

We found a small table upstairs away from prying ears so we could discuss things more privately. I could not help but smile; he was so handsome, and his eyes sparkled. I knew I was in trouble, but I was enjoying his company. He was wearing a checkered shirt and dark black jeans. I could see the hair on his chest poking out from the buttons that were undone at the top. The waitress then came over with a tray and handed us our drinks. Jack poured two sugars into his coffee.

"Not sweet enough, then?" I joked, trying to lighten the mood.

"So, what are you going to do?" Jack quipped back.

"What do you want me to do?" I asked, trying to gauge his feelings.

"You can't keep it. If I was your age, it wouldn't be so bad, but I can't look after a baby, I'm too young myself."

I knew how he felt; we were not stable and were both too young.

"I feel the same."

The look of relief came across him like I had never seen. I was so frightened to be in this situation, but at the same time knew that there was no way we could keep the baby. We chatted about what to do next with me agreeing to book into a clinic, as I knew I was too far gone to have the abortion pill. After around an hour Jack closed the conversation and got up, saying he had to be somewhere to look at a new car. I was feeling hurt and asked if he would like some company.

"No, it's OK. Take care and speak soon." He leaned over and kissed me on the cheek. I got into my car and cried. He had made me feel so unwanted.

5

The next day at work I could hardly focus. I kept making mistakes and daydreaming at the window, lost in thought about the baby. My boss, John, seemed to sense my distraction and asked if everything was OK. I said I needed to take an early lunch break and bolted out into the car park. I logged onto the internet on my phone and found a local clinic to talk to about the abortion. I cried the whole way through the call, knowing how awful this truly was, but feeling it was the right thing to do. Eventually it was booked in. I texted Jack to tell him the time and date. *"Thanks x"* he replied. He was being so cold and distant, I hated it.

"You out tonight?" I texted Felicity, seeing as it was a Thursday and our usual night out. I decided I needed a drink to forget about my problems.

"Ah, not tonight mate, I'm skint," came the reply. Damn.

"OK, not to worry," I texted back. It was too much to text about what was happening, and I just wanted to block it all out, so I decided not to tell Felicity. I knew that our friend Nicole was usually out, so I messaged her to see what she was up to.

"Yeh, come around mine and get ready together before we go out if you like?"

"Sounds perfect," I replied. I then went back up to the office and tried to shake this feeling off and get on with work. The hours went by slowly, but I fully engaged in what was needed of me in the office. When 5 p.m. came I couldn't get out the door quick enough.

At home I cooked myself some pasta and I took a shower and went through my wardr⟨ a knee-length polka dot dress and black heel in a bag, ready to go to Nicole's. Nicole only 1 away and the walk to her house did me some good. I was ⟨⟩ for a night out.

"Hi, come in, fancy a wine?" Nicole said as she opened the door, shoving a glass of white wine in my hand before I could say anything.

We tried on a few outfits, but I ended up wearing the polka dot dress that I had brought from mine with a slim-fitting red belt. We giggled away as we did our makeup together and sipped wine. Finally, we were ready, and it was time to get into the taxi to go to the club. I had told Nicole nothing about Jack or the baby, deciding the fewer people that knew about it the better and I could try to forget it was happening.

We paid our entry into the club; it was Thursday and was student night. This meant it was a bit of a dive but always a cheesy, fun, and cheap night out. Nicole was a popular girl and knew lots of people, so was always darting off to talk to someone, leaving me standing there with a drink in my hand. It wasn't ideal given the situation I was in. I was getting more and more drunk, ashamed of how others would perceive my carelessness if they really knew. Nicole mouthed, "There's Liam!" and went off to speak to him.

Nicole and Liam were seeing each other, and I wondered if Jack would be with him. Out of the corner of my eye I saw him standing with Steve and a group of lads. I hung about in the background, aware of how having a bottle of alcohol in my hand would look. Jack gave me a scowl. I wanted the ground to swallow me up, so I ran into the toilets.

Jack followed me in and aggressively questioned what I was doing.

"*Nothing,*" I replied angrily.

He stormed off and went back to the bar. I stayed in the

ets for a while longer and poured my drink down the sink, not wanting to taste the drink or be associated with it while I was still pregnant, and my head was all over the place. What was I doing?

After a few minutes, I came out of the toilets and saw Nicole dancing with Liam, who was grinding into her back in time with the music. Nicole was laughing and clearly enjoying flirting with him. Someone pushed past and knocked my arm. Looking up, I realised it was Jack and I smiled. He smiled back and apologised. "Are you having a good night? It looks like Nicole and Liam are!"

"It's OK; I'm not really sure why I am out. How about you?" I replied.

"No, me neither. Do you fancy getting out of here?" Jack winked, placing his hand on my bum and pulling me in toward his crotch. Once again, my heart melted—he need not say any more; I was like putty in his hands!

Once back at mine, Jack eagerly slammed the front door shut. I led him upstairs and he ripped my dress off, tenderly kissing my neck and moving slowly down to my stomach. Stopping there, he looked up at me and I nodded to him that it was OK. He carried on and grabbed my hips, pushing my tummy into his face and working his way ever so slowly down to my knickers. I could not believe him; he was adamant that I was to get rid of the baby but would come back for more and not even say a word about it. Maybe I was thinking too much into it, but him kissing me right there felt purely like a dig at me, as if he was rubbing it in my face.

He pushed me onto the bed and put my legs above his shoulders, sliding a finger inside me, rhythmically getting faster and faster. I could not contain myself and reached down and placed him inside of me. The feeling of his bare skin inside of me was turning me on so much that I told him I was close to orgasm. "Me too," he replied. I dug my nails into his hot, sweaty back and moaned with delight as I felt him come deep inside me. He lay on top of me for a while, then moved off me. I suddenly felt very vulnerable but strangely close to him at the same time. I turned around and curled up into his arms, then laid my head on his chest. It was a nice, fleeting feeling of contentment. I was smitten and he knew it.

In the morning, Jack woke me up early, saying he had to get home as he had work. I pulled on some jogging bottoms and a hoodie, scraped my hair back in a ponytail, and we went down to my car.

On the journey home, he asked me what time the procedure was, knowing it was in two days. I told him it was at 11 a.m. and asked if he could attend with me, knowing full well I'd already texted him the details before.

"I can't babe, I have work!" Jack replied.

I couldn't believe it—I had already told him the details, but he had not found time to take the day off work! I was literally seething.

We drove back to his house in silence. I had nothing more to say to him. I felt wounded by his lack of regard.

"Bye, babe," he said and kissed me on the cheek.

"Bye, gorgeous," I replied as he shut the door. I drove away in a daze and couldn't help but cry. My emotions were all over the place with him.

6

The day of the abortion came. I had already told my mother about the baby, and she immediately offered to come with me for the procedure.

I hadn't been able to sleep so I got up early to get ready. I was waiting on the sofa with the TV blaring when I heard a knock on the door. I peered through the curtains and saw Mum waiting on the doorstep. I immediately went to let her in.

"Hi," I said, giving her the tightest cuddle possible, needing that comfort and reassurance.

"Oh, Louise, let me in first!" She laughed, prising my hands off her as she stepped inside.

"Sorry, Mum, I'm just so pleased to see you. I didn't sleep well at all."

"I can imagine. I hope you are feeling OK?" she asked as she took her jacket off and settled down on the sofa.

"Ah, I don't know. It's a life-changing decision, isn't it? I know it's for the best though, I just can't help wondering what life would be like if I kept it. I know it would be hard, and Jack would possibly run a mile, but it's still something I can't help but think about."

"Of course you can't. That's just a natural reaction, Louise. Try not to dwell on the what-ifs. You've made your decision together, and you were adamant it was the right thing to do the other day. How would you be able to support the baby? You both need to want it, Louise."

"I know," I said, tears rolling down my cheeks as I leaned

in and hugged her once more. "I just want to know that it is truly the right thing to do. It's such a horrible thing to do though, Mum. I don't want to end a life and I really do like Jack."

"Louise, it is a horrible situation, I understand, but you made your decision, and I will be here with you every step of the way. I know that you and Jack are not in a steady place right now and that you both feel that a baby would be a burden on your life and relationship. You said yourselves that you can't give a baby what it deserves at this moment in time. It wouldn't be fair on the child, and I certainly can't look after it full-time."

"I know, Mum, I know," I said, continuously crying, wiping the tears from my cheeks and trying to compose myself.

"You will get through this, Louise, I promise you." Mum hugged me tighter, stroking my hair as I sighed, hoping she was right.

"Come on then, let's go." I pulled away and wiped the final tears off my face.

"OK, ready?"

"As I will ever be," I stated, grabbing my coat, bag, and keys.

The journey seemed to take forever even though it was a little over forty minutes away. I stared aimlessly out the window, feeling as if I was in a dream and not talking to my mother. I just never thought I would be in this situation, and I was annoyed at myself. I knew the consequences, but just did not think it would happen to me. As we pulled up to the car park and Mum turned the car engine off, I knew it was now or never.

"How are you feeling? Are you OK?" Mum looked over at me, carefully tucking a piece of my loose hair behind my ear in that gentle, caring, motherly way. I knew it must be hard for her to watch me go through this and make this decision. It would, after all, be her grandchild if I went through with the pregnancy.

I looked over at her and smiled. "Yes, it's the right thing

to do given the circumstances, isn't it?" I asked, hoping for approval once more.

"You've talked this over with Jack, and that's what you both decided. Now come on, let's try to put this day behind us as quickly as we can." Mum squeezed my hand, smiling reassuringly.

The procedure was over quickly, and Mum drove me home, ensuring I was OK. I just felt numb. I felt guilty about having an abortion as it was something I had always said I would never do.

Once back at home, Mum settled me down on my bed and tears rolled down my face. "It's OK, sweetheart," she exclaimed, hugging me tightly. I was so lucky to have her in my life. Never judging and always accepting me for me.

I had told her all about Jack and, true to herself, she had not formed an opinion, keeping an open mind as usual. Once she had gone, I texted Jack to say I was home, and that I was OK. I was upset that there were never any concerned texts from him asking how I was or wishing me luck throughout the day. I was so cross at myself for believing he was a better person; I was upset that it was over; I was upset that I had done something I vowed never to do in having an abortion; and I was upset that it was now over between Jack and me. My feelings were all over the place and my body ached.

"*OK, thanks for letting me know. x,*" Jack finally replied. I wondered why that was all he had replied—was that all I had been worth to him? I put my phone on silent and cried myself into a deep sleep.

7

The next morning, I woke to find a text that had been sent late the night before from Jack asking if he could come over. I was still angry at him but part of me wanted to see him and hug him. I went downstairs and poured myself a large mug of steaming hot coffee and stared out into the garden. A tiny blue tit was tapping at my window frantically. The minute I went over to the window, the bird flew away. I sat back down at the kitchen chair and sipped my coffee; the bird came back again. *Tap, tap* it went. I was not rushing as I had booked the day off work, unsure of how I was going to feel after the operation. *Tap, tap.* Again the bird flew back as if to get my attention. I watched the bird in amazement and somehow it lightened my mood. I realised how small I truly was in this huge, mysterious world.

I typed Jack a message. *"Hey, sorry I've only just seen this as I fell asleep early last night. Would have liked to have seen you though. X."* I put my phone down and went to clean myself up in the shower. I was bleeding heavily, but at least the pain had subsided slightly.

After I got dressed and then dried my hair, I checked my phone and saw a text message and missed call from Jack. I opened the message.

"Would you like me to come over this afternoon? My shift finishes at 1pm. I could take us out for lunch if you like? X."

My head was telling me not to agree but my heart could not resist, and I wanted to see him so badly. I immediately called him back.

"Hey, I've just read your message. It would be great to meet up, yeh."

"How are you feeling?" Jack responded.

"I'm OK, a little sore but OK all things considering. Did you want to pop here after your shift then?"

"Yeah, let's go out for lunch, my shout. I'll be over about 1.30 p.m."

And with that, I decided I had better start getting ready to look my best for the date.

At exactly 1.30 p.m., the doorbell rang. I looked out of the window and saw Jack's BMW outside. I re-checked my makeup in the mirror, grabbed my thick grey winter coat and bright red bag, and rushed to open the door.

He was sitting in the car, smiling at me. "Get in then, babe," he shouted through the open window. As I opened the door to the passenger side of the car, I realised he was beaming from ear to ear at me. It was such a welcoming, sweet smile and immediately put me at ease. I truly felt that things were going to be OK.

"Where are we going then?" I asked.

"Never you mind, all good things come to those who wait," Jack joked, leaving me none the wiser.

The car whizzed along, and we found ourselves at a small country pub called The Fox. It was nestled between a large woody common and a river.

He parked and turned to face me. "Are you sure you're feeling OK?" he asked, genuinely concerned.

"Yes, I'm OK."

He leaned over and kissed me. The all-too-familiar feeling swept over me, and I felt like a child in a sweet shop, gazing at everything I had ever wanted, amazed that it was there in front of me in one place. I knew he was all I would ever want, but hated to admit it to myself.

We clambered out of the car, and I narrowly avoided stepping in a puddle. Jack opened the entrance door to the pub and ushered me in. "What would you like to drink?"

"Just an orange juice please," I replied. "Shall we sit outside, admire the view?" I urged. Even though the pub was quiet I just wanted to be alone.

"Sure, why not."

It was a crisp, cold day but the sky was bright blue and inviting. We chose a wooden picnic bench on the edge of the garden as close to the river as we could get. Two vivid white swans slowly swam past us. It was a magical, truly romantic, and peaceful setting. I looked up and smiled into his warm eyes. If I could have bottled this feeling I would have. I knew I was in love.

The afternoon passed by, and we decided to go back to mine to watch some films together.

It was a pleasant and dreamy evening cuddled up on my sofa watching reruns of *Friends*. Jack kept me relaxed and made sure I had drinks and snacks available. He was acting the perfect gentleman.

I was bleeding heavily, and he gave me painkillers to soothe my stomach. "I'm sorry I put you in this position, Louise. I should have handled the situation better," Jack said, passing me a glass of water to wash the painkillers down and kissing me on the forehead as he did so.

Feeling cared for I looked up and smiled at him. "It's OK, it was me as well. I should have been more careful, and I completely understand why you would not want to keep the baby too."

"It's not that I hated the idea. It's just that I have so much more life to live. I'm too young. There are things I still want to do. I'd also rather be in a better financial position to bring a child into this world. I honestly did think about this, Louise, but I'd be lying if I said I had wanted to keep it right now."

"I get it, I really do. I agree that we are not in a financial or stable enough position to bring a child up. I also agree that you are too young, myself included really, I guess. I still hate that I've done that though. It wasn't my proudest moment that's for sure!"

"Louise, don't feel bad. I respect you and your body so much for what you have gone through and please believe me how sorry I am for putting you in that position. I care about you. I care about us, but it would be the wrong thing to do. You know that, surely you can feel it too, can't you?"

"Yes, I can. It's still such early days for us."

"It is. I am enjoying getting to know you more and I don't need that upheaval in my life right now."

Looking at his face, I could see the pain behind his eyes. Knowing that I was in control of his destiny and the worry that I would change things was too much for him. I moved my face closer to his and gently kissed his soft lips, losing myself in the moment and enjoying feeling him close to me, gaining warmth from his body.

He eventually pulled away, smiling. "You really are something else, you know that don't you?" he said.

"Why thank you! Likewise." I winked. "So, what other things do you have in mind that you need to do?" I tried to lighten the mood, realising I wasn't going to get much more out of him than what he had just given me.

"Ah, travel. There are so many places that I'd like to see. I'd love to see more of the USA, all sorts really. How about you?"

"I've not thought about it, to be honest. I guess I've just been coasting along. Although I do like visiting new places and sunnier climates of course!"

We laughed and joked, and Jack told me more about adventures that he would like to pursue and of previous holidays that he had been on. He certainly was a free spirit.

At 11 p.m. Jack said he was going to go home as he had work early in the morning but wanted to make sure I was OK to go to sleep. I snuggled into bed, and he let himself out, kissing me on my forehead once more before he left.

As I drifted off to sleep, I realised I had seen a different side to him: a loving, gentle side, which only added fuel to the fire in my heart. Although what had happened was terrible, I fell asleep that night feeling more content than I had in such a long time and knew that I had done the right thing, for both of us. He really did warm my body in more ways than one.

8

Back at work, my reports had piled high, and I was eager to get them completed. I was feeling more stable and breezed in through the office toward the kitchen to make a cup of tea to get the day started. It was someone's birthday and as usual they had brought in cakes for everyone to share. I had never really got this; it was your birthday, yet you were supposed to bring treats in to share? Surely everyone should be treating you. It did not make sense to me, but who was I to complain on a day like today when all the yummy gooey treats were laid out in front of me?

While the kettle was boiling, I stared out the window and released a big sigh. What did the future hold, I wondered. Jack seemed to be my only outlet lately, and I knew I needed to get a grip.

A few weeks passed and I got stuck into work. Calls were constant and the report typing was getting absurd. It was a great distraction, and I tried my hardest to forget about Jack as it just didn't feel like he was as interested as I was or that it was going anywhere. I really didn't want to get hurt again.

I had been chatting to Karen, who had opened up about her personal life and her interest in spirituality. Karen had talked me through some fun clubs that she belonged to, and I decided I would finally like to join her for a trial that evening.

Karen and I drove to a small village half an hour away in a quiet cul-de-sac on a very ordinary-looking road. We pulled up slightly early and Gwen opened her front door, welcoming us in. Karen and Gwen hugged, and we went into her sitting room. The room was painted in plain magnolia with cream leather sofas, all very safe and not what I had envisaged for a psychic's house. I sat down on her sofa and chatted about the journey. She brought out some exercise paper and asked us to write answers to the questions she was asking us about our lives.

At the end, Gwen rounded the papers up and spoke to me softly, saying that she could see me with a man, a man who would steal my heart and make my soul ache.

"This man has dark hair and dark eyes. He has tanned skin and he is charming—it's almost as if he pulls you into him. You cannot resist him. I see you falling hard for him. I can see him travelling, travelling to many unusual places. I can see you both having fun together, laughing and kissing. Lots of chemistry here." She laughed. "He has a sister. That's right, one sister who he is close to. I can see a future with this man. He needs to grow up slightly. He rushes into things, and doesn't think of the consequences or people's feelings too much. I can see underneath that he is a good person who wants to do well, but he's immature. He wants fun in his life right now, but you will be with him."

I instantly felt that she was talking about Jack. It made the hairs on the back of my neck stand up, and I had goosebumps all over me. I was intrigued and I asked her to go on.

Gwen said that this man was going to play a huge part in my life, but it was not always going to be easy or a straight run. What she was saying resonated with me so badly and I just knew that Jack and I would be together eventually, even if the road was rocky, or at least that's what I hoped for.

I looked back at Karen and realised that she was thinking the same thing as me. "It's Jack, isn't it?" I squealed. "I just know it."

"It does sound familiar, doesn't it?"

"Well, spirit never lies," Gwen replied, smiling at our excitement.

9

A few days later, one Friday evening I was visiting my parents' house for dinner straight after work. I was sitting chatting with my mother when my phone beeped. *"Hey, how are you? What are you up to?"* It was from Jack.

"I'm OK, just having dinner with my parents then going to chill tonight. What are you up to?" I replied. I could feel Mum tentatively looking at me; she had probably guessed who was messaging me.

Jack immediately replied. *"Just about to go to the pub with work."*

What was he up to, I wondered, and left it at that, assuming he was just being friendly and trying not to think too much into it.

Quite soon after, he texted again and asked if I wanted to meet up. I must have been grinning at my phone as Mum asked what was up. "Oh, Jack has asked if I wanted to meet up tonight," I replied.

"OK, well just be careful, Louise. I know how easily these boys can pull you in. It reminds me of that song, you know the one, with the lyrics about how big brown eyes can hypnotise you." We both giggled, knowing what a sucker I could be at times.

I replied, *"Yes, OK,"* half thinking he would cancel and trying not to get my hopes up.

Jack then asked where I wanted to meet, and I suggested on neutral grounds at a pub in a couple of hours so that I could go home and get myself glammed up! Half an hour or so passed then I received a reply to say that he was still in the town where he worked and was going to stay there for a few more drinks but asked if I wanted to meet him and his colleagues there. My heart jumped! Jack had never introduced me to his family or work friends before. I immediately jumped at the chance and agreed.

"Dinner's ready. Where do you want to sit?" Mum alerted me back down to earth.

"Umm next to Dad, over here." I scoffed the meal swiftly because I wanted to get back home and start planning what to wear.

I kissed Mum on the cheek as I left. "Thanks for the delicious meal, Mum, I will call you tomorrow, and don't worry, I'm back on the pill!" I laughed, knowing that she wanted me safe and knew she would want to hear how it had all gone.

"No problem, my love, you go out and have fun. Stay safe." She kissed my cheek and said goodbye.

10

As I pulled to a stop outside the pub, I double-checked that I was in the right place against the address he had given me. I texted Jack to say I was outside, and he replied straight away, asking me to come in. Checking my reflection in the rearview mirror, I established that I looked decent enough to meet him and his colleagues and that my coat was covering my modesty.

I had decided on wearing one of my all-in-one, high-legged lacy black lingerie sets with black heels and a grey wool smart Ted Baker coat over the top. I had minimal makeup, so from the outside I guess I looked like any other office worker and hopefully would fit in. I wanted Jack hook, line, and sinker and had done my best to entice him in, hoping a glimpse of the lace underneath the coat would keep him wanting me.

I locked the car, crossed the road, and pushed the heavy door wide open. I immediately spotted Jack propped up at the bar. He was wearing a white shirt with green stripes and smart dark chino-type trousers. He looked up and smiled that welcoming, innocent, broad smile of his. I knew I was in for a pleasant evening and my heart skipped a beat.

"Hey, you OK?" He beamed at me, kissing my cheek and grabbing my hips toward his. "What would you like to drink?"

I looked around and everyone seemed to be drinking alcohol but as I was driving, I decided on a lemonade. It looked like a celebration of some kind with nearly the whole office in tow.

"Lemonade please, gorgeous!" I smirked.

One of Jack's colleagues came over and introduced himself to me. "Hi, I'm Paul, you must be Louise?" Paul offered his hand to me.

"Hey, lovely to meet you, Paul!" I shook Paul's hand as he grabbed it, pulled me in, and kissed my cheek. He was friendly, relaxed, and I could tell he was a bit older than Jack. "So, what are you two lovebirds up to after this then?"

"I umm, I umm, I'm not sure," I replied, tugging my coat closer to my body, suddenly feeling self-conscious that I was wearing nothing but lingerie underneath in this overcrowded bar.

"Well, a few of us are heading into town to a nightclub. If you wanted to come and join us, it will be a laugh."

"Hey babe, here you are" Jack came back from the bar, passing me my lemonade, and stood between me and Paul, shoulders back and chest out like he was marking his territory. It was clear that he was uneasy leaving me to talk to Paul.

"Paul has just invited us to go onto a club after this if you wanted?" I asked, eager to find out how Jack would respond.

"I think we are both tired, you know, early night for us," Jack replied, winking at Paul then grabbing and pulling me toward his chest. I could not help but giggle; it was endearing how he was so obviously trying to be one of the lads but at the same time obviously not comfortable in the situation.

"OK, no problem. The offer is always there, buddy," Paul replied casually.

I could almost hear Jack sigh with relief. I knew he just wanted to get back to his so we could be alone and have sex, but I was enjoying being out with him and it was almost teasing him in a sense. I found it fun.

"So, what do you do for a living then, Louise?"

"I work for a firm of lawyers as a PA. It's all very dull," I replied nonchalantly.

"Interesting." I could tell Paul had not really thought it was interesting at all.

He then went off to talk to his colleagues and Jack and I discussed our day. I loved how his eyes sparkled and he looked so innocent when we talked, like he hung on my every word. If I thought about it hard enough the signs were there that he was younger than me, but behind closed doors he made me feel like I was the inexperienced one and that he was much older. He was dominating and in control.

"So yeh, I quickly got changed into something special and came out to meet you, and yeh, here we are!" I exclaimed, telling Jack all about my day while fiddling with the buttons on my coat, trying to leave a glimpse of bare flesh out here and there.

Suddenly I felt a hand on my shoulder. I turned around to see Paul again. "You know, Jack, you really have gone up in my estimation, young fella, your girlfriend is hot! How did you manage to pull her?" he said, smiling at me. "She reminds me of that TV presenter back in the 80s, you know the one—Michaela Strachan, that's it!" he chuckled.

Girlfriend?! The fact that he had called me Jack's girlfriend made me squeal with delight inside. What had he been telling them about me? I couldn't help but laugh. I remembered Michaela well and knew I looked nothing like her, but it was funny all the same. If I hadn't known better, I would have thought that Paul was hitting on me. He was more in my age range than Jack, but there was no way I was going to give up Jack for anyone, I thought to myself as I finished the last drop of lemonade off. I looked around and could see most of the pub emptying as people went off home or into town.

"No, I can't recall who she is, probably too long ago for me, bro. Right, are we off then? Did you want a lift into town?" Jack asked breezily.

"Yeh, if the lady doesn't mind driving me there, that would be great. I can't wait to have a dance. Are you sure you don't want to join us?"

"No mate, you're alright, not tonight."

We all piled into my car, and I was nervous about driving in front of Paul especially as he was so outspoken, but I knew my way and managed without any incidents.

"So, then, you two lovebirds, how long have you been together?" Paul asked as I fell silent.

"Not too long," Jack replied, keeping his cards close to his chest.

"Louise, how old are you if you don't mind me asking?"

"I'm twenty-four, why?" I replied, worried that Jack's age was going to become an issue.

"Wow, I thought you were around nineteen too, but a mature nineteen-year-old."

"Haha, are you joking? No way, it's completely the other way around. I am the immature one, and he's the mature one out of us most of the time." I laughed. I respected Paul's directness and was interested to find out what Jack might have told him about myself and our relationship.

"So, where do you two see yourselves in two years' time?" Paul eagerly asked.

"Hopefully with a ring on her finger and still with me," Jack blurted out, patting my hand on the gear stick and giving me a wink. I swerved the car in shock, almost hitting the curb. I was so stunned. I had no idea how to come back to that comment and I could feel myself getting hotter with embarrassment.

Luckily, we were nearly there. I pulled up outside the nightclub, and Paul leaned over to kiss me goodbye on my cheek. "Have fun, you two lovebirds," he said as he got out of the car, slamming the door shut.

"Yeah, see ya!" Jack laughed sarcastically.

I leaned over and kissed Jack full on the lips, still high from what he had just said.

"It's so good to kiss you again," he declared.

I unbuttoned my coat further down; I wanted Jack to see what I had on underneath. He reached over and put his hand on my thigh, slowly going higher until he reached my knickers.

"Are you actually wearing anything?" he asked, taken aback.

"Of course," I said and opened my coat fully.

"Wow, I wish I had known. We could have sneaked off earlier, you dirty cow!" Jack replied.

"Right, let's get going then," I said and immediately drove off in the direction of Jack's house.

As soon as I pulled up into the driveway, I turned the engine off and went to get out of the car when he pulled me and grabbed my face, kissing my lips like he needed me there and then.

Once inside, we crept upstairs slowly and quietly so we didn't disturb Steve. Jack closed the door gently behind me and pushed me into the door frame. "Ouch," I giggled as he reached down and placed a finger inside of me, teasing me.

"Am I the best lover you have ever had?" Jack asked in a way that suggested he didn't really expect me to reply.

Cockily I replied, "Am I the best YOU have ever had, young man?"

"Yes, by far, you were made for me. I have missed this so much. Hmmmm," he groaned. "You are so good." He unbuttoned his jeans and rhythmically stroked his bare, hard cock whilst I stood motionless, back against the door, taking in every breath and adoring him.

All I could think about was having him inside of me. He turned me on even with his eyes, sparkling in subtle innocence, staring at me like I would be his last meal, as if he were hungry for my body. It was his eyes, his beautiful hazel eyes.

When I was with him, talking to him, kissing him, sleeping next to him, I felt undeniably in love. I was warm, happy, joyous, and all was content with the world.

"Over there," he ordered, pulling me toward the bed. "Take that coat off now."

Eager to please, I did as I was told and slowly unbuttoned the coat, placing it neatly on the hook behind the door, wiggling my bottom as I did, knowing he was eyeing my every move. Feeling confident in my lingerie and heels, I turned around, flicked my hair, and straddled him on the bed. I lifted his chin and kissed and sucked on his bottom lip, tasting his warm saliva and feeling his rapid breath on my face, ensuring that I was doing enough to tease him, pulling back when he pushed in further for more.

"Stop that." He laughed, pushing my knickers to the side, and continued to pleasure me whilst I groaned, loving every second.

"You like that, don't you?" he asked, again more of a rhetorical question. I smiled and bent over, placing his beautiful cock inside my mouth, looking up at him, twisting my body so that he could continue to play with me.

"You are back on the pill again, aren't you?" he asked, getting things straight in his head.

"Mmm," I replied, my mouth full of his deliciousness.

"Stop, I don't want to come yet." He pulled at my hair, moving my face up and away from him. "Let me get inside you. I want us to come together."

After we finished, we snuggled up and fell asleep, bodies entwined in a hot, sweaty mess. I woke up early as the sunlight drifted through the windows. It was like a huge weight had been lifted off me and I had released any stress that I was carrying. I was on a high, floating with the clouds.

II

"We had sex for two hours, Felicity! I mean, two hours!!! I have carpet burns on the tops of my feet for goodness' sake!" I had met up at Felicity's flat the next evening and relayed the story back to her, giggling at every aspect. Jack had reduced me to acting like a teenage girl.

Felicity had laid out two bowls of chips for us and rested them on her coffee table next to a cup of tea and some forks. The chips were steaming hot, and I squirted ketchup all over them, diving in. "Thanks, babe," I mumbled, mouth stuffed full of chips.

"So, do you think you will see him again soon?" she asked bravely.

"Well, he did ask me what I was up to at the weekend, and I had said that I was doing nothing. So yeh, hopefully we can meet up again!" I beamed.

"Oh, you didn't, did you?" Felicity knew this was against *The Rules*, a book that she lived by. It was a set of rules/instructions that girls were meant to follow in order to get the man of their desires. You were meant to act like you did not like them and let them do all the chasing, book your diary up in advance so you could not be tempted to see them on a whim. It was a stupid book, something from out of the 1950s, no doubt.

"I want to see him, Felicity! There is nothing wrong with that, surely. I'm just being honest; I don't want to play games this time. Besides, he said he was going to a festival down the coast and if he had time after he would love to come and see me."

"Well, don't hold your breath, Louise."

"No, I won't, although it would be nice. He's so dreamy!"

"Ugh, you make me sick, he's so dreamy," Felicity mocked as she threw a chip at me. We giggled together, laughing at how ridiculous I had become and so eager to please him. I was not acting myself one bit and Felicity knew.

The rest of the weekend had gone by extremely slowly. I had not heard from Jack and was going out of my mind trying not to contact him. I tried to keep busy and went out for a long walk that Sunday, keeping my exercise up and getting fresh air. I hadn't gone out drinking that Saturday night and needed to get away from my house and thoughts.

Monday came and still nothing from Jack. I started to feel angry. I thought he might have texted me at least! Whenever we were together it felt like we were a couple and whilst having sex it felt like we were in harmony with a real connection. But yet again, here I was, days would go by and I would not hear from him. To say I was in a bad mood at work was an understatement.

I had told Karen about our rendezvous the day after it happened, so I decided to let her know I still hadn't heard from him.

"I just don't get it. He let me meet all his work friends! I wouldn't do that unless I was serious about someone." I sighed.

"Of course he did, he just wanted to show you off, Louise! To prove that he could have someone like you and to fuel his ego. You really are too good for him."

"Oh, I don't know, I'm definitely not perfect and neither is he. We just seem to click when we are alone. It's all this uncertainty that I hate. I'm just me, I don't play games, what you see is what you get, and I feel like he's playing me." I sighed, slumping back into my chair, feeling overcome with emotion and defeated.

"Come on, let me make you a cup of tea, then you had

better get on with that file for John before you lose your job!"

"Thanks, you're a star. I don't know what I would do without you." I jumped up, giving Karen an almighty embrace. I knew I had a lovely work family and was pleased to be getting busy again.

12

Jack eventually messaged me a week later. *"Hey babe how are things going?"*

I was ready to let rip at him, furious about the lack of contact and emotionally exhausted from worrying. Instead, I held back and pretended things were fine, just like *The Rules* suggested. I waited an hour and then I replied. *Oh, Felicity would be proud*, I thought to myself!

"Yeh, great thanks, how are you? How was your weekend?"

"It was awesome, the festival was so good, I was completely mashed!"

Ugh, what a waster! I hated the fact that he had gotten so drunk and out of it that I had not been on his mind. Men can be so different from women—in fact, the more drunk or out of it I got, the more that I wanted to see or speak with whomever was on my mind!

I was pleased that he had finally got in contact with me, though, and I wanted to see him, so I made plans to meet up the next evening. I arranged to pick him and Steve up from the train station after he had been at a work's do in London, and then go back to his.

I parked the car in the train station car park and waited until his train came in. I immediately got out of the car as I saw it pull up and watched Jack get off the train alone. I called out to him, pointing to where I had parked.

He came over with a huge smile set on his face and leaned across, planting a soft kiss on my lips. "How's my gorgeous girl doing?"

"Gorgeous, eh? Why thank you!" I laughed, my heart beating at the fact he had called me his girl.

"Can you go over to the van; I really fancy a kebab if that's OK?"

"Yeh, of course," I replied, driving into an empty office car park and parking close to the kebab van. We both got out and walked to the back of the queue. While waiting, Jack pulled me in close to his body and kissed me passionately. I reached down and felt he was already hard. He laughed and tugged at the button on my jeans, pulling it toward him, looking down. "No knickers, I like it. You saucy little minx." Jack sucked the air in through his mouth as if he was holding back.

"All for you, babe, all for you," I replied, winking at him, hoping that he liked the idea.

There was a group of lads in front of us in the queue at the kebab stand, and they turned around to see who was walking up toward them. One of them was undeniably staring at us, and I noticed Jack stood up taller and inherently stuck his chest out. He then put a protective arm around my waist as if to mark his territory. I knew he had been drinking, but he was constantly giving out mixed signals, like, I know he fancied me but was sex all he wanted?

Soon enough, it was our turn to get to the front of the queue. The other lads moved to the side and waited for their order to be cooked. Luckily neither side said anything, although they continued to stare at us. I felt a warm glow inside, knowing that he felt protective over me, or at least wanted to show the world I was his. *If only he would tell me that himself*, I wished to myself, getting caught up in the moment.

Jack grabbed his order, and we walked back to the car. "You OK?" he asked as I put my seatbelt on.

"Yeh, why wouldn't I be?"

"I'm not sure. Those lads were definitely checking you out."

"Haha, really, I hadn't noticed. I was too busy feeling you up." I laughed and reached down to stroke his crotch.

"Mmm, that feels good."

"Hold on, let me move the car a bit." I quickly moved the car away from the queues and pulled over at the back of the car park, by the tree-lined boundary, as Jack continued to eat his kebab, stuffing it in his mouth hurriedly, like it was his first meal of the day.

"There, that's much more private for us both." I leaned over and started undoing his jeans, looking him straight in the eye and waiting for him to get hard again. I looked up and out the car window and saw there was a security camera directed at us.

"Looks like we're being watched, babe," I said, motioning to the camera in the corner. "Let's give them something to look at, shall we?" I laughed, smiling at the thought of someone watching Jack and me, and them also getting turned on. I bent down, placing his stiff, pulsing penis in my mouth, and he squirmed in the seat as I got nearer and nearer to him orgasming. I loved being in control of his emotions; it gave me my power back after all the times he had been so in control of our relationship.

"Stop," he groaned. "Let's finish this back at mine. We've got to go and get Steve too."

I laughed and sat back in my seat. "I can't wait! Where are we picking him up from again?"

"Just at the train station, he caught the later train but should be here soon."

"OK, let's go back and wait for him there then."

It wasn't long before Steve's train pulled up.

"Hey, Louise, thanks for this!"

"You're welcome."

Jack pulled the seat forward and let Steve climb into the back.

"OK, I think I know where we are going from here," I declared and turned the music up, singing along to the lyrics as I drove hastily to Jack's.

Their house was only about ten minutes away and I parked neatly, grabbing my belongings out of the boot. Steve went in first, clearly drunk and stumbling on the stairs, laughing loudly to himself. I hung back and let Jack lead the way. We said good night to Steve and then went into Jack's room.

I sat down seductively on the edge of the bed, fiddling with my extremely tight, black satin corset top, ensuring that my boobs were popping, and it was placed in the most perfect position for Jack to want to seduce me. I loved the fact that Jack already knew I was not wearing any knickers under my jeans and was hoping that he too could not wait to be alone with me and have some fun.

I looked up at him as seductively as I could, wishing he would come over and seduce me. I placed my bag on my lap and rifled through my makeup, pulling out my red lipstick and applying it in a small handheld mirror, temptingly looking at Jack out of the corner of my eye, carefully applying the bright red, luxuriously creamy lipstick to each side of my lip as if my life depended upon it. Sucking in my breath, just waiting for him to come over and touch me. I felt electric and was sure he could sense my tension.

"Well, I have been waiting to be able to do this to you. Now come here." Jack finally turned around and pulled me by the arms toward him, kissing me on the lips. Unbuttoning my jeans, slowly and gently sliding them down over each hip and down past my bum, he tossed them to the side of the room. Jack being Jack, and more focused on my pussy and bum, he left my corset alone.

He positioned me in the middle of the bed, grabbing at my wrists and placing me exactly where he wanted me, carefully moving my limbs in the correct position whilst looking up at me, smiling. I sat quietly, eager to please and moving without fuss, wondering what he was up to, staring into his lush, soothing brown eyes.

"You have certainly made me want all of you tonight!

Coming to pick me up in this outfit, no knickers and boobs sprawling out the top of your bustier. Now let me do what I want, or I will spank you and you won't like it."

"Is that a demand, or are you asking me?" I teased as he cocked his head to one side, winked his eye, and tutted at me. Always subservient to his every need, I sat still, waiting for him to tell me what to do next.

He then aggressively pushed me and turned me over, forcing my head onto the bed, smothering me into the pillow so I could hardly see or breathe. He slapped me forcefully on the bum. "Do you like that?" he said, more of a statement than a question.

"Do you like it?" I replied, twisting my head to the side and looking up at him, teasing and wiggling my bum up in his face, wishing for him to just enter me. I was already getting turned on by the thought of him inside of me, fitting my body like he was made for me.

"Of course I do." And with that he licked his finger and steadily squeezed it all the way inside me, beckoning in a backwards and forwards motion whilst slamming my head back down into the pillow, forcing his torso heavily down upon my naked body, ensuring he was leading at all times.

"Your turn to tease me now, is it?" I laughed, turning my head and looking over my shoulder whilst he fingered me harder. "Seriously, just put it inside me, babe. I want you."

Jack let go and fumbled at his jeans, unzipping them and pulling his boxer shorts down to uncover his glorious manhood once again.

"I'm going to fuck you so hard, you dirty little bitch," Jack shouted aggressively, pushing me further into the bed, and then onto all fours as he rammed his throbbing rock-hard penis straight inside me. "How do you like this now? No teasing from me," he laughed.

I physically couldn't speak even if I wanted to. His hand was pushing down on my head and I could barely move, let alone answer him. He thrust himself back and forth, getting deeper and deeper into me, groaning and firmly squeezing and pulling, ripping at my butt cheeks, exposing every orifice of my body whilst reaching up every now and then at the lace on my corset, teasing it open slightly.

Eventually I managed to wriggle free from his grip and sat upright.

"No, you don't. I will take control from here," I exclaimed, watching his handsome face light up like a kid in a sweet shop. Turning him over, I climbed on top and placed his penis inside me once more and slowly, rhythmically moved up and down, ensuring I was the one in control this time. I rested my hand on the top of his head, grasping at his thick black, glossy hair. I could feel myself getting wetter and wetter, getting more absorbed into the moment as I felt my hand slip down his beautiful face to his chin and then down around to the bottom of his neck as I gripped tighter and tighter. Horrified at what I was doing, I looked him in the eye and realised that he was smiling. He actually liked it! He was literally something else, never failing to surprise me. I laughed, loosened my grip a little, and continued to bounce upon him.

Faster and faster I rode upon him, realising that he was watching my every move, feeling like his eyes were staring straight into my soul. He had a glint in his eye that I found fascinating. He was so sexy, he turned me on just by being himself, and knowing he was enjoying what I was doing to him excited me.

I cupped my breasts, which were still half-covered in the smooth satin corset, slipping my nipple out from my right breast, ready for Jack to squeeze and caress. Always in tune with each other, his hand reached up and teased his finger around my nipple slowly with an almost feather-like touch, making it stand out and erect. I let out a moan and couldn't help but push him deeper inside me with each breath, uniting our bodies in this glorious rhythmic motion.

Almost immediately, we came together in a blissful moment of heat, sweat, and passion. I slowly moved off his torso, allowing his soft penis to drop out of my dripping-wet vagina. I wiped the cum off my thigh with my hand as I walked to the toilet, on cloud nine.

I couldn't help but wonder what had just happened between us. He was becoming more controlling, and I wasn't sure how to take it. I knew that I was falling deeper and deeper for him and the sex was unreal between us, but there was an unnerving feeling that he was holding back on something or that things might escalate in a way I might not like. What happened if he had been playing it safe with me this whole time and had some serious dark and strange fetishes that I didn't know about? I really wasn't sure if I was going to be into anything dark or strange. I knew I loved sex and risqué behaviour, but I didn't feel like I had any other fantasies that needed to be played out. Although, sadly, I knew I was smitten with him and possibly wouldn't be able to resist anything that he asked me to do, even if I hadn't agreed with it or really even wanted to do it.

I was slightly nervous at the thought of all this, but I pushed those thoughts to the back of my mind, splashed my face with ice-cold tap water, and returned to bed. Kissing him on the cheek, I then turned over, wrapping the covers all around me, engulfing my body in the cosy, soft duvet as if floating on air after such a euphoric moment between us.

The next morning, I woke to find Jack placing a cup of tea and some hot, buttered toast on the end of the bed. "Wake up, babes, I've made you some breakfast." He stood over me looking innocent and pure. I could not help but laugh at the situation.

"Jack, that's super cute. The first boy to make me breakfast. I love it." I reached up and kissed his lips tenderly, swiping the toast as I leaned over and checked the time on my phone. "We better get ready. I've got to be at work in forty-five minutes, and it's across the other side of town, shit!"

"Yeh, no problem, anything you need?"

"I'm OK, I think I've got everything, I just need a quick shower," I replied as I got up and headed to the bathroom for a freshen-up.

13

"You're bright and cheerful today." Karen smirked at me as I hung my coat on the back of the office door.

"Oh really? Hmmm, it must have been my brilliant evening last night then. Would you like a cup of tea?" I endeavoured to spill the beans ever so casually.

"Oh no, you didn't see Jack, did you?" Karen tutted.

"I did, and he was a real gentleman this time!" I beamed.

"Come on then, tell me what happened. I know you're desperate to."

"Karen, he was utterly divine! Honestly, I feel like I am in love. He made me breakfast in bed this morning, after our night of passion." I winked at her. "I am just going to go to the kitchen to get a cup of peppermint tea and I will be right back. Hold that thought!"

"Louise, you are a devil." She laughed.

I could not help but shimmy down to the small white kitchenette at the back of the office with a genuine spring in my step. I thought it must be obvious to the whole world that I'd had a great night last night. As I boiled the kettle, I thought about how much I had enjoyed Jack's company, and not just the sex. He could be so kind when he wanted to be.

"Right, I am all ears," Karen declared as she patted the chair nearest to her. I grabbed my mug and began relaying the previous evening's shenanigans from start to finish.

The week went by in a flash with work extremely busy again. I was still on a natural high from my and Jack's last evening together and life seemed effortless in this mood. I was happy to stay behind and work on the reports that John had given me, and I felt unstoppable.

Friday, lunchtime came and a group of us decided to go to the local pub for lunch. It was a sunny day and we grabbed a couple of benches outside in the garden and pushed them together so we could all fit. Most of us came for the social and didn't drink any alcohol, but sometimes a bottle of wine would be offered up. Just as I sat down, I heard a familiar beep from my phone alerting me to a new text message. It was Jack. Eagerly, I opened the message.

"Hey! How's it going?"

"All good here, how are you?" I replied, anticipating where this might be going.

"Why don't you come out tonight, I'd love to see you."

Not much notice, yet again—why was he like this? He just assumed I'd either have nothing planned or that I would drop everything to see him. Gosh, he was right though. I couldn't wait to be with him again. It was like a drug and I was hooked.

"What do you have planned? I was going to visit Felicity," I lied.

"Come on, come out. I'm going out to celebrate my cousin's birthday. You can stay at my sister's place with me and have some drinks. It will be fun."

I put the phone back down and considered the options. I wanted to see him but also did not want to give in so quickly. He knew I was putty in his hands. Beep went another message.

"Sorry, no pressure, but of course I'd love to see you," the text read with a wink emoji at the end.

"Oh go on then," I replied, already having butterflies in my tummy, nervous at meeting his sister as I knew they were so close and I had heard lots about her.

"Let me guess, Jack?" Karen nudged me.

"How did you know?"

"By the huge grin on your face. Louise, you are a sucker for him, aren't you? You haven't heard from him all week.

What does he want this time?"

"He's invited me out tonight."

"Are you going?" I could feel the rest of the group look up from their menus and eye me inquisitively.

"Yes, why not. I want to see him, and he did message me first," I replied curtly, as if that had made things alright. I was trying hard not to be so eager with him, but I always caved in when he got in touch.

"OK, well I hope you both have fun. Let's order!" Karen swiftly changed the subject. I guessed she was getting a little tired of hearing about him and me moaning that he was so hot and cold. It was true, I hadn't heard from him over the week, but as I had poured myself into work, it wasn't a problem.

"I think I will have the falafel and spinach wrap with chips, oh and an OJ. What about everyone else?" I looked up from the menu, deciding that I would be the one to go to the bar and order for everyone this time. We usually set up a tab for this kind of thing and then split the bill at the end. It wasn't often that we came out, but it was such a nice, small family-run business. We all got along and when we did get together, we always had a laugh.

The evening came, and I decided to dress casually, opting for a more demure look in light of meeting Jack's sister. Jack had told me to meet him at a little village pub that I had been to once or twice before and so I parked around the back of the pub in an open car park. I texted him to say I was there, locked my car, and looked up through the windows of the pub. I could clearly see him standing up reading a message on his phone. He came out with a beer in his hand.

"Hey!" he shouted. I did all I could not to run over to him and give him a huge hug. Holding back, I tried to act cool.

"I knew it was you. I could spot those legs anywhere," Jack teased as he approached me and then lifted my chin up toward his, placing a soft, gentle kiss on my lips.

"Will my car be OK here overnight?" I was worried.

"Yeh, of course, I've left mine here plenty of times. I will take you back to it in the morning. Come on, let's go in." Jack took my hand and led me in. The pub was bustling and noisy. I felt uncomfortable and out of my depth, seeing as I had not had a drink yet. Jack introduced me to his sister Gabi and then went to the bar to get me a vodka.

"Hi, Louise, it's great to finally meet you," Gabi said, reaching over, kissing me on both cheeks and giving me a hug. I immediately felt at ease with her. She was a small-framed girl and had the same thick, dark hair as Jack that hung straight down to her shoulders. Gabi's skin was paler than Jack's, but she had a friendly smile with welcoming, sparkly dark brown eyes.

"Hi, Gabi, likewise," I replied, taking in the warmth of her embrace. She was sitting with a large group of people, took my arm, and introduced me as Jack's girlfriend. I was astonished—what had he been saying to people about me and why was I not aware that I was his actual girlfriend? I certainly did not feel like his girlfriend even though I wanted nothing more than that.

"So, you are the girl that has finally turned Jack's head then?" Gabi said to me, pulling up a chair next to her and patting it, gesturing for me to sit there.

"Oh really? What has he been saying about us then?" I laughed.

"All good things, don't worry. Just how much he likes you and that he's always looking forward to seeing you."

"Likewise." I blushed. "We have a lot of fun together and he's so very different to any other guy I have ever met. Yeh, I do really like him," I replied, knowing that Jack was within earshot of our conversation, realising that this was my chance to subtly let him know that I cared about him more than just for sex.

"So, what do you work as?" Louise asked, taking a sip from a bright blue cocktail with multi-coloured straws hanging out from the glass.

"I work in a small office as a PA to two lawyers. It's all very dull to be honest, but it pays the bills. You know how much house prices are around here!"

"That's nice. I know what you mean about house prices, they are extortionate, aren't they? I live down the road, but I am only renting. It's convenient and close to work for me now, but I'd love to own my own home soon."

"Oh good, it's such a lovely area here too. What do you do then?"

"I'm cabin crew. I work for B.A."

"Wow, you must have some stories to tell," I exclaimed as I leaned in closer and rested my chin in my hands to hear all about it and get to know Gabi some more.

The night went on and Gabi and I continued to chat, getting to know one another. Gabi was a sweet girl and although two years younger than me, we did have lots in common and got on well. My nerves subsided and I eased into the conversation.

Jack eventually came back and placed my drink on the table. "You two seem to be getting on well," he declared as he stood behind us and placed his hand on my shoulder in a manner that said he was claiming me as his.

The night went on without a hitch and we continued to drink, laugh, and joke, wishing his cousin a happy birthday. The barman rang the bell for last orders. "Shall we head off now? I'm done!" Gabi declared.

"Me too," Jack answered, standing up tall. I looked around and realised that we were the only group left in the bar and apart from us, it was now quiet. I grabbed my bag and staggered to the door, trying my best to appear sober but giggling loudly as I did so.

We were all drunk when we got back to Gabi's house as she clumsily opened the door and we followed her in, both stumbling over the threshold behind her. I slammed the door shut and looked around. It was a cosy terraced cottage near the village centre. You could tell that Gabi had recently moved in as there were still boxes strewn around the house and walkways.

Jack then took my hand and pulled me around the corner away from the front door and into a bedroom. The walls were plain white, and the carpets were cream-coloured. There was just a double mattress with white bedding on the floor pulled to the side next to the radiator. It was clean and minimalistic.

No sooner had I stepped foot inside the room than Jack sat on the bed and started pawing at my dress, running his hands up my legs, pulling me in closer. He reached the top of my thigh where he slowly slid my knickers to the side and teased my clit. He was so forward and always knew what he wanted, I thought to myself, allowing his hands to wander wherever he wanted.

"Oh yeh, expecting something, are we?" I laughed.

"Of course, now come here and give it to me. Right now," he demanded.

I slowly unzipped my dress to reveal my bright fuchsia-pink lace bra and matching short-style knickers. I wiggled around to show off my derriere and tease him.

"Get here now!" he shouted.

Taken aback, I immediately did as I was told. I was already getting turned on, anticipating us riding together and becoming one. Jack unzipped his jeans, pulled them down, and took his shirt off, tossing them to the far side of the room. He lay back on the bed, his hard-on visible on the outline of his body against the moonlit sky outside. He took my hand and motioned for me to take my knickers off. I straddled him, leaving my beautiful bra on, rubbing my hands over my breasts, teasing him some more.

I lowered my hips and sat upon him, resting my wet crotch on the very top of his erect penis. He looked me deep in the eyes and then suddenly rammed himself all the way inside of me. "How does your tight little pussy like this then?" Jack whispered as I gulped. I looked down and watched our bodies together, in and out, rhythmically, his magnificent cock covered in my juices. I loved being with him.

"I feel like your body was made to fit me," I panted.

"Me too. You're incredible," Jack replied as he came, his hot fluid dripping down my thigh as I moved positions.

I kissed him on the cheek and walked to the bathroom. I stared at myself in the mirror, examining myself and wondering what he was thinking about—us, me, and our situation. I cleaned myself up and climbed back into bed, where we both fell asleep cuddling. I was in heaven in his arms and fell asleep with a big grin on my face.

I was woken up early with the sunlight pouring in through the bare windows. "Jack, let's get up and go move my car. I've got to get to work," I said, looking at the time on my phone, wanting to just get home and shower with all my belongings around me.

"OK, OK, give me a minute," he replied, turning over and wrapping the duvet back around him.

"No, Jack, come on. I've got to go into the office to get the papers ready for John's seminar on Monday. Remember, I told you last night?"

"Yeh, OK." Eventually he got up and threw on some jogging bottoms and a hoodie. I put on the clothes I was wearing the night before. We went out the front door quietly, closing it behind us so we would not wake Gabi. Jack drove me to my car in silence and gave me a peck on the cheek as I left.

"Thanks, babe, see you soon," I said as I got out of his car.

"See you soon," he replied and drove off, as if in a hurry to get somewhere. I felt a bit lost, feeling like he had been distant this morning. I tried to shrug it off, telling myself that he was just tired, hungover, and cold. He probably just wanted to get back into bed and chill. That was it, nothing else to it, I was sure.

14

I got home and immediately turned my shower on full blast, the hot water burning out in what looked like a puff of smoke. I got undressed and stepped into the bath and under the shower, letting the water trickle over my face and dampen my hair, letting last night's memories wash away down the plug hole, freshening my head and trying to rid the ache I felt from too much drink last night. I quickly pulled out a skirt and jumper and placed a slice of toast in the toaster, pouring myself a mug of coffee to wake myself up on the way into the office. I didn't want to be late and mess this up for John and, even though there were only a few of us meeting at the office, I wanted to be on top form.

As I pulled up into the car park, I could see that everyone else was already there. "Well, better late than never," I said to myself as I reversed into a space. "Let's do this."

A couple of weeks passed by, and once again I had not heard from Jack since our last meeting. I had told Felicity and Karen all about it, and both were as baffled as I was and couldn't work him out. I felt like they were slowly getting fed up hearing about it and tried to hold back on information so as not to bore them.

I couldn't help but think about him constantly, though. It was consuming me; I wanted him, I wanted to see him. I kept going backwards and forwards as to whether I should contact him. One minute I was like, yeh, do it, the next I was talking myself out of it, saying to myself that he wasn't into me in that way and just wanted sex. Eventually, I decided to pluck up the courage to text him and ask how he was.

"All good babe, all good," he replied. No asking if I was OK or furthering the conversation.

I was confused yet again and embarrassed that I had made the first move. I knew I was acting like a child, but with him I was subservient no matter how hard I tried to man up!

"Did you want to meet up soon?" I proposed.

"Yes, I would love to see you. How about tomorrow evening for dinner? I can pick you up around 8pm, make sure you dress to impress!"

"Oh, sounds perfect. I can't wait," I replied, wondering if he would have actually texted me if I had not initiated it. He was hard to work out—I never really knew how he felt about me. All I knew was that I craved him, both his body and mind. It was like he was my addiction.

At work I tried to concentrate as best I could even though my tummy was doing summersaults just at the thought of seeing Jack again. I was confused. I knew I had fallen for him and knew that I wanted to make a life with Jack, but he was so hard to read. Was he just interested in sex? Was he seeing other people? Was he like this in his previous relationships and was I just expecting too much too soon? I sighed, not knowing any of the answers.

𝓁

The doorbell rang and I ran down the stairs, grabbing my coat and bag as I went. Jack opened the car door for me. "There you go, Louise," he said as I sat down and he closed the door. I had no idea where he was taking me. All I knew was that it was somewhere for dinner and that I had to dress up like he had told me. I had decided on wearing my tight, black, high-necked minidress with long sleeves and my black patent sandals. The dress was body-con style and super tight, so I needed to wear it without any knickers, or my indented knicker line would show. Also, partly more to the point, I knew that Jack would love the thought of me going out without any on, and I could not wait to see his face once he realised. Straightening my hair to almost an inch of its life and completely overdoing my eye makeup with a lashing of mascara and eyeshadow accentuating the shape of my eyes, I felt as ready as I ever would be.

"So where are we going?" I tried to find out.

"Just you wait and see." Jack winked at me as my heart did a flip. He could turn me on with just a smile, I swear! I decided to tease him and moved my seat back further, jutting my legs out in front of me. I then placed his hand on my thigh. He immediately took it back to change gear without noticing my knicker situation, so I decided to up the game and hook my skirt up, opening my legs just enough for him to notice out of the corner of his eye.

"Are you not wearing any knickers?" Jack laughed.

"No, I can't. The dress is too tight! It looks better this way."

"Damn right it does," Jack said as he slowly moved his hand up my thigh. I already wanted him inside me. Eagerly, I pulled at his hand again and placed it on my vagina. Jack slowly brushed his fingers up and down, getting me excited. I wanted him right there and then!

"Oh, Jack, you know how to get me going, don't you?" I whispered, not wanting him to stop.

"Not now, you're so naughty, Louise!" he replied and took his hand away to change gear and slow down.

We pulled up on Kensington High Street, London, and found a parking space. "Here we are, babe. Kensington Roof Gardens!" Jack declared.

Oh my, we were going to Kensington Roof Gardens! I could not quite believe it—what a great venue.

I got out in awe of the building, excited to get in and see what it was like. I grabbed at Jack's arm and pulled him in close, smiling from ear to ear.

Once in the restaurant, Jack pulled the chair out for me to sit, kissing my neck as I did so. The waiter came over. "What would you like to order for drinks?" he asked.

Jack winked at me and blurted out, "Whatever my girlfriend wants, I am happy to share."

My heart floated and butterflies danced around my ribcage. I would have given anything to have been his girlfriend.

The waiter came back and poured us each a glass of champagne and left us to examine the menu. At that moment, I looked around and could not believe how I felt like the luckiest girl alive. Jack was everything I wanted and every moment I was with him was a joy. *Clink* went our glasses as we raised a toast to each other. Under the table I rubbed my leg up and down his shin, waiting for him to flinch, as I knew the games were about to start. I twirled my finger around the rim of the glass, smiling and staring into his eyes. He moved his foot to mine, and I wrapped a leg around his, pushing my body closer to the table to get closer to Jack. I opened my legs wide as he lifted the other foot up and slowly skimmed my leg, resting it on my inner thigh. Even the thought of him getting hard, wanting and needing me made me wet.

I moved in closer still and took a large gulp of my drink. "I think I need to go to the ladies," I whispered, winking as I got up, looking over my shoulder to see his reaction.

Jack did not disappoint. A minute later he followed me into the empty toilets where we located a suitable cubicle. "Here," Jack demanded as he pushed me into the corner, wedging me up between the wall and the door. He then carefully slid my dress up over my hips and slowly traced his fingers along the outline of my vulva, teasing me with the tip of his fingers, getting me more excited and in turn wetter. I gasped, wanting him inside me immediately, so I tugged on his shirt collar, pulling him closer toward me, kissing his soft, full lips and urging him to hurry up and pleasure me to the max.

I reached down and felt his hard manhood beneath his

trousers, and began rubbing him, ensuring he was as hard as he could be. I started to unzip him whilst putting my other hand inside his pants, feeling his warm cock and noticing he was already pulsing. Fully unzipped, I wrapped my hand around his penis, sliding it up and down, looking deep into his eyes.

I grabbed his right hand and placed it on my pussy, bending and twisting his fingers so that he was ready to enter me and knew I needed him to continue pleasuring me whilst I bent down and placed him inside my mouth, licking and sucking on the end of his beautiful cock, sucking any drops that had escaped the further he become aroused.

He pushed his middle finger deep inside me, beckoning in a backwards and forwards motion, moving my thighs apart with his wrist, pushing deeper and feeling every inch of me.

I moved my face away from his penis and looked up at him. He grabbed at my hair, pushing my head down again. "Don't stop," he ordered me. Smiling, I did as I was told and continued to suck, lick, and move in rhythms, enjoying feeling him get closer to orgasming whilst he slipped another finger inside my already soaking vagina.

Suddenly Jack shouted "Stop!" and pulled on my hair, raising my head.

"I want to finish inside you now," he ordered.

I obeyed and got into a steady position, balancing my back against the wall, realising that the door could open if we were bouncing against it. I spread my legs as far as I could and positioned him so that his penis was just touching the tip of my vulva. Staring, smiling deep into his eyes, I kissed him and pushed him slowly, carefully inside me, pushing his bum toward my body, ensuring he was as deep as he could get in this position. I gulped as he managed to push it further, breathing heavily into my ear, the heat coming out of him and giving me goosebumps across my neck and down my body.

I loved the thought of my juices dripping all over his beautiful bare cock, so I let myself go, enjoying his breath becoming quicker, thicker, and fuller. I kept my hands cupping his bum, digging my nails in deep, pushing into him, becoming one.

We fucked hard and fast in the dark and confined space, banging our bodies against the walls as I screamed with pleasure, unable to contain the satisfaction that I was feeling from his body once more.

Jack moaned, kissing my bottom lip, biting it until he drew blood! I pulled back and stared at him. He didn't blink, only continued to push in and out of me and we both finally came together in a sharp, loud, burning desire of crescendos surrounding us as if we were the only people in the building.

Panting, he pulled himself away from me, his limp penis sliding out of me, completing what we had set out to do.

We both rearranged our clothes as if nothing had happened, and I wiped down my thighs, dripping from his hot semen, trying to clean myself up but loving the thought of some part of him still inside me.

"Jack, that was brilliant as always," I said, planting a kiss on his cheek as he zipped himself up. I wiped my hand along my bottom lip, checking the back of my hand for blood.

"Likewise, gorgeous." He laughed. "We were lucky no one came in and found us."

"I'm not sure you would have stopped anyway!" I winked at him.

Laughing, we separately exited the cubicle, stopping to wash our hands and smirking in the mirror as we did so, feeling completely fulfilled.

Back at the table, we proceeded to review the menu whilst giggling to ourselves. The other diners were unaware of our recent sexual rendezvous. We were just so lucky that no one had come in, although I thought that it would have certainly made it more interesting.

"Back now, are we Sir, Madame, ready to order?" the waiter asked.

"Yes, all sorted now, thank you. Are you ready to order, babe?" Jack replied matter-of-factly, pointing to his chosen dish, looking directly at me.

"Yes, let's order." I smiled. "I'll have the spinach and ricotta cannelloni, please."

"I will have the steak, medium rare please," Jack replied, handing the menus back to the waiter.

The food came out quickly and was divine. We laughed and chatted, got to know what one another had been up to lately. It was wonderful.

We drove home together with my hand in his lap. Every now and then I would glance over at him and smile. We were extremely naughty together, but it certainly made life interesting. I loved every minute I had with him; I had unmistakably fallen in love.

"You know I love being with you, don't you, Jack?" I asked. "Not just for the sex. I love the way your mind works."

"I know you do babes," Jack replied sassily. I wondered why he had not said he enjoyed spending time with me too. *Oh jeez, men are so difficult to read*, I thought to myself as the car zoomed in and out of the bends turning left then right, and eventually, straight down my road.

"Are you coming inside?" I offered, knowing we had not discussed him sleeping at mine, but I had hoped he would.

"Yeh, of course," he replied, switching the engine off and getting out of the car. I fumbled for my door keys in my handbag. They were, as usual, right at the bottom. I grasped them and turned the key in the lock, pushing the front door open just as Jack came up behind me and softly kissed my neck. I could smell his sweet breath and wanted him all over again.

With Jack, I knew I was insatiable. It was like the more I got, the more I wanted. I just wanted him to thrust himself inside me all the time. I wanted him to brush my hair away from my face and fuck me—raw, animalistic sex. I wanted to be riding him for hours, and for him to leave me aching, exhausted, the whole works. I was completely and utterly infatuated with being with him, near him, having him inside me.

I knew it was not healthy to feel this way, but I couldn't help myself. I was out of control. It was not like me at all and I often wondered if the reason for wanting to have so much sex with him was related to that feeling of closeness or to create a bond with him, and the only way I was getting that from him was through sex.

I tried not to dwell on the whys and hows; all I knew was how I was feeling, and I was enjoying being with him. It was, however, unfortunate that he often went quiet, and I couldn't help but worry that he had gone off me or met someone else that he preferred. I often thought that it was like he knew exactly what he was doing, pulling me in just that little bit, teasing me and giving me enough attention, but not so much that I got bored. He was clever and, in a wicked way, it made me want him more, knowing he was playing games with me. I knew this was messed up, but again my feelings took over and the highs I felt when I was with him were so incredible that I was willing to sacrifice the deepest lows just to be with him as much as I could. He was like a drug; I couldn't seem to stop.

15

Buzz buzz, the alarm went off at what felt like the middle of the night. "Right, babe, I've got to get up and go to work. I've got some papers that I need finalising ready for Monday," Jack declared.

"That's OK. Shut the door on your way out." I nudged him with my leg, teasing him. I could peek out from the corner of the duvet and see him get up and throw his clothes back on and couldn't help but smile.

He leaned over and kissed my cheek. "I'll call you later babe, OK?"

"I'll look forward to it, gorgeous. Hope you get everything done." I quickly pulled the duvet back over my head to keep the warmth in. I fell back into a deep, comfortable sleep.

Later that morning, I called Felicity and arranged to meet her for a catch-up that evening. I felt like I hadn't had quality time with her recently and wanted to catch up with how she had been.

I stayed in the car and tooted my car horn outside her flat. I looked up and watched as she opened her bedroom window, shouting down that she would still be another five minutes.

I sat there thinking about the next time I might see Jack. I had hoped he might come over to mine for dinner, maybe I could cook for him, or we could choose takeaway together. Have a casual night, then hopefully some more hot sex after!

"What are you smiling at?" Felicity said as she got into the passenger side.

"Oh, haha, I hadn't realised I was smiling, but if you must know, I was thinking about when I might next see Jack."

"Oh, you're so boring going on about him! Can't you talk about anything else?" Felicity laughed and poked me in the ribs. I loved her honesty, her vibrancy. She never sucked up to me or let me get away with anything. It was so refreshing these days with the woke culture.

"Yes, let's talk about your love life then. Had any more dates?"

"Yeh, er, hmmm. Maybe go back to talking about Jack then." She smirked, placing her hands over her face. She hated giving anything away, preferring not to be vulnerable.

We had planned to go to a local pub to sit and chat. I drove through the town centre, which was busy for a weeknight. "Shall we just go to the usual? It looks busy."

Felicity looked at me with a twinkle in her eye. "Yeh, why not!"

"Fab, I'll go round and park up," I said as I pulled over to an open-air car park. "Free parking after 6 p.m., so all good!" I motioned to the signpost by the pay and display machine.

We walked into the pub and I took a good look around, trying to see if there was anyone I knew there. We went straight to the bar. "I'm driving so I'll have a soft drink. What about you?" I asked Felicity.

"A Bud if that's OK, mate?"

I ordered the drinks and then we went to sit down outside where Felicity could have a smoke and we could get a decent catch-up in. It was so nice to just be out and chatting with her. I filled her in with what I had been up to with Jack and my work, and she shared some of her recent dating dilemmas with me. I felt like I had missed a lot and I knew I must make more of an effort.

"Cheers, gorgeous," I said as we clinked glasses, celebrating our friendship.

16

The next evening, I had organised to cook for Jack. I decided on cooking chicken and pasta, nice and easy, with a side order of prosecco to lighten the mood!

The doorbell rang at exactly 7 p.m. as we had arranged. "Nice one, Jack!" I said to myself, pleased that he was taking it seriously. I opened the door and he handed me a huge bunch of white lilies. "Thanks, babe, come in," I offered, sniffing the flowers. Their scent seemed to already be consuming the hallway.

Jack came in and gave me a quick, sharp kiss on the cheek. I took his coat and ushered him into the sitting room, ready to wait while I continued dinner. "Fancy a drink while you are waiting, babe?" I asked.

"Sure!" Jack replied, taking the remote off the coffee table and settling down on the sofa. I went back to the kitchen and poured two glasses of prosecco.

"Here you are." I leaned over and handed one to Jack. He placed it straight on the coffee table and pulled my arms toward his body. I bent forward and straddled him as he held onto my arms tightly, kissing me passionately in a way that made me feel like I could have had him there and then. "Stop it! Wait!" I laughed, pulling myself off him. I straightened my clothes and went into the kitchen to dish up.

"Right babe, no funny business. I want you to enjoy this," I said as I positioned his dinner on the table. "Do you want more prosecco?" I asked, pouring it anyway, hoping that he would be staying the night.

"Erm, ha, yeh, OK then, cheers!"

I let Jack tuck in first, hoping that he would like it, nervous as I hadn't cooked for him before, although I knew that if he didn't like it he wouldn't tell me!

"That was delicious," Jack announced, rubbing his tummy. "What is for dessert then?" He winked at me as I cleared the plates away.

"I am! Let me finish up here and I'll be back in a sec." I placed the plates in the kitchen and practically ran back to sit next to him, moving over onto the edge of the sofa, making room for him to squeeze in beside me. I took the remote and turned the volume down low so we could talk and poured us both another glass of prosecco.

"So," I proceeded. "Tell me, is there anything that you have wanted to try sexually but haven't had the opportunity to do yet?" I asked, looking him straight in the eye as I seductively ran my finger up his thigh. "You know I would do anything for you, don't you, and I mean anything!"

"Well, most guys love the idea of watching their girl fuck another man. I have had a threesome before, but I imagine having one with you and another girl would be awesome. I'd love to have her bent over, licking you whilst I enter her from behind. I'd love to watch your face as she made you come with her tongue."

I nearly spat my drink out on the floor. Where had that come from? I was thinking more along the lines of using handcuffs or making a video of ourselves having sex, you know, something more generic!

"Wow, well that's a mighty tall order, babe." I gulped. "What type of girl would you like to see me with?" I continued to tease him, stroking his leg, running my nails along the hem of his jeans, trying to warm him up, tickling at his ankles.

"I don't think I'd mind, so long as she is clean and pleasing you," he replied.

"Well, how about I organise something for us then? I might just know the perfect girl, or even the perfect couple." I knew that if I was going to do anything like that it would have to be on my terms. One of my old colleagues, Kieran, was such great fun. We still chatted from time to time, and I knew that he and his wife were into this sort of stuff. If it meant pleasing Jack, then so be it—I had always said I would do anything for him and I knew that I would.

"I'd love it. That sounds fun. I know it would be for your pleasure too, but boy would I enjoy it."

"Haha, I'm sure you would, but Jack, this would be all for you. I'd organise it as a gift from me. It's not really my sort of thing." I felt compelled to help him achieve his dreams, especially if it involved me being with him too. Besides, it could be fun!

"You're in," he said, smiling, clasping my mouth and cheeks with one hand, aggressively pulling me closer toward him. Kissing me urgently, he pulled my top down with his other hand, squeezing frantically at my breast like he needed me then and there.

I pulled away and bent down to unbuckle his belt. He pulled his arms up and rested them behind his head, smiling knowingly at what was about to happen. I opened his jeans and pulled them down to his knees, reaching into his boxer shorts for his hard penis, noticing that there were already small wet droplets forming at the end of his penis. I positioned it in my mouth as he grew bigger and harder whilst I caressed the tip every so often, letting the length go all the way inside my warm, wet throat, clasping all his girth. I wanted to feel every inch of him inside me.

I stood up and took my jeans off, closing the curtains as I did so. Pushing my knickers to the side, I placed him inside of my already wet pussy, driving him deeper and deeper all while Jack was sitting there smirking with his hands behind his head like a lord and master, getting his just deserts.

Suddenly, he moaned and a gush of liquid came inside me.

Knowing he had come, I slowed down and got off of him. He ushered me onto the sofa and spread my legs, bending down and licking at my clit, sucking it, tasting his semen mixed with mine as I climaxed on his face.

"That was quick and to the point!" I laughed as he moved up, wiping his lips on the back of his hand. I shuffled up and grabbed my jeans that were strewn on the floor.

"I couldn't resist. You were leaning over me looking so fine and I just wanted you. Is that such a bad thing?" Sometimes, just sometimes Jack could be open with an almost innocent quality about him. I knew full well that he was the one in control and leading me astray, almost coercing me at times. But occasionally he looked at me with such warm, welcoming, beautiful big brown eyes that my heart skipped a beat, and, in that instant, I felt a huge connection.

"No, quite the opposite. I love that you want me." I did the final button up on my jeans and sat back on the sofa, snuggling up in the crook of his arm whilst he flicked through the channels for a film for us to watch.

I must have fallen asleep in that position as the next thing I knew Jack was wrapping a blanket over me, kissing me goodbye. "I'm off now, babe. Speak to you tomorrow. Thanks for dinner."

"Oh." I sat up, wondering what time it was and why he was leaving. "Aren't you going to stay the night?"

"No, I'm better off getting home so I can get up for my early shift tomorrow. Is that OK?"

"Course it is. I'll see you out, babes." I got up and wrapped the blanket over my shoulders, shivering as I did so, feeling the cold chill of the night. Following his lead, I looked in the mirror in the hallway and wondered where my makeup had gone—it looked like it had literally slid down half my face! *That's most likely why he didn't want to stay the night*, I thought to myself. "Bye, gorgeous," I said, kissing him goodbye and locking the front door behind me, ready for a good night's sleep.

17

"Karen, would you like a cuppa? I can fill you in on all the goss," I said to Karen as I hung my coat up on the back of my office door the next morning.

"Why do I get the feeling this is going to be a long catch-up?" Karen laughed, rubbing her chin.

"No idea," I said as I grabbed her cup and went to the kitchen.

"So, where shall I start... I also want to know what you have been up to!" I pulled the hard plastic office chair next to her and placed her hot coffee on her desk.

"I haven't been up to much lately; I've been to the circle group a couple of times and that's been interesting. You should come along again!"

"I'd love to! Let me know when you next go. I've been seeing a bit more of Jack."

"Look at that smile on your face. You are smitten!"

"Argh, I know. I hate it but love it at the same time. I do feel a little out of control with my feelings to be honest." I took a short, sharp breath in and Karen looked up at me, trying to work out what I was getting at.

"Go on."

"Well, when I am with him, I feel a sense of peace and ecstasy. He's just unapologetically himself and I love that about him. I almost admire him, you know? He's not judgemental and always thinks outside the box. He is exciting, handsome, and great in bed. He's also very unpredictable, though, I'm well aware."

"Well, yes, there is that, and he hasn't been the most reliable to date, has he?"

"I don't know, Karen. I believe in him, I truly do. I can't put my finger on it, almost a gut feeling. He came round mine last night and I cooked dinner for us both. We had such a sweet, cosy evening." I sat there reminiscing about the evening before, although I couldn't help but wonder why he had left and not stayed the night.

"Well, just keep in mind that he's unpredictable. Are you sure that is not what is pulling you towards him? The excitement of it all?"

"No, it's more than that, although of course, yes, he is exciting." I winked. In the distance I could hear my office phone ringing. "I had better get back to my desk before John wonders where I have got to. I don't need him on my back!"

"Of course. Let's finish this over lunch? My treat! We can go to the Royal Oak round the corner if you like?"

"Yes, thank you. I'd love that. I was going to go to the gym, but my gosh you have persuaded me."

"Fab, about 12.00 noon then?"

"It's a date!" I shimmied into the office next door and settled myself down for a full day of typing reports. Checking my missed calls, I could see that John had already phoned, so I dialled his number and called him straight back.

Before I knew it, it was midday. I was eager to get outside and breathe in some of the fresh air, have a proper catch-up with Karen and get things off my chest. "I'll drive, yeh?" I said as we left the building.

"That would be nice, OK, thanks," Karen replied, and I pressed the button on my keys for the central locking to open so that we could get straight in. I pulled up to the pub and the car park was almost empty. Picking an easy spot, I parked up.

"Fancy a glass of wine?" Karen asked.

"If you are having one, then yes, why not!" I exclaimed.

We picked a wooden bench in a bright sunny spot outside.

Feeling the warmth of the sun on my face, I began to relax and asked Karen about her dating life.

"Oh, don't ask!" she replied. "I thought I had a good thing going with Nick, but he eventually turned out to be a sponger."

"What happened?" I asked as the waitress brought our drinks over with the lunch menu.

Glancing at the tattered and worn menu, Karen declared, "I fancy a jacket potato, how about you?"

"Yes, classic beans and cheese will do for me!" I replied.

"Great, I'll get them in and I can fill you in when I get back." Karen got up and went back to the bar to give our lunch order. We only had an hour break, but it was so nice to just get out and have a chat.

I gazed at my phone and decided it was time to send the feelers out to Kieran, asking if he and his wife Sierra were free for a bit of fun sometime soon.

I had known Kieran for a few years; we had met at my previous job working for a firm of solicitors that dealt with personal accident claims. It was a large firm and he worked in the call centre for the claims department as the first point of call, speaking with clients and taking their details to pass on to solicitors. I was a PA to one of the directors but was back and forth obtaining information from his department. We soon struck up a friendship and kept in touch. The job was kind of a stop-gap job for him as he really wanted to go on to be a firefighter. For the time being Kieran was just having a bit of fun, earning some cash and getting out and about before he settled down. He was my age, handsome, smart with a tall, athletic stature.

Kieran also had an air about him that was fundamentally virtuous, a standing pillar in the community you could say. Underneath all that, once you got to know him better, he was devilishly naughty and a complete sexual deviant. Although I had never slept with him, he had been on at me for years to meet up with him, but I had taken it all as banter, knowing we were better off as friends and knowing what a joker he was. Time had passed and he had gotten married, but we remained friends that spoke just a few times a year.

By all accounts Kieran and his wife were part of a swinger's club and often hung out at a members-only nightclub in London where couples went along and swapped partners, allowing others to wander about and watch them all have sex. I just took it all in jest and enjoyed hearing all the stories— never in a million years would I have considered meeting up, yet here and now, the time felt right, and I couldn't imagine doing this with anyone else but Kieran and Sierra.

"*So, how about this meet up then, fancy it with my man too?*" I texted, knowing to get straight to the point as Kieran liked.

Usually, Kieran was slow at responding, so I put my phone back in my bag and carried on with my lunch. I told Karen nothing of this arrangement as it almost felt like a dirty secret, mine and Jack's secret at any rate. Although I couldn't help but smile—who knows, it could be fun!

Later that evening, I got a call from Jack. "Hey, how was your day?" He sounded calm and interested in what I had to say. We chatted about how our day had gone and discussed meeting up at the weekend. "So, any more thoughts on organising what we were talking about last night?"

"Ha, yes, I had actually. Where shall I start?"

"Tell me everything!" Jack insisted. I then proceeded to tell him about Kieran and how I had already instigated the first text.

"Well done that girl! I'm excited!"

"Haha, good, I aim to please!" I knew I had him where I wanted him and that this was going to be a huge effort on my part to see this through. I felt anxious and completely out of my depth, but if it meant getting closer to Jack, then so be it.

18

I stood there staring at myself in the mirror, happy with the outfit I had chosen. I wanted to feel sexy and in control and wear something that was easy to take off. I had been through my wardrobe and decided on a beautiful ankle-length black dress with splits down the side and a lace panel around the midriff. The dress was tight and hugged me in all the right places. I teamed it with some pillar box red high court shoes, and matching vivid red lips.

We had arranged to leave mine at 7.30 p.m. I looked at the clock on the wall: 7.20 p.m. Nearly time. The taxi should be here any moment. My stomach was doing summersaults. I wasn't sure if I was doing the right thing, but I was never one to go back on my word and I knew how much this would mean to Jack. I just wanted to please him in any way I could, even if that meant betraying myself in the process.

I heard the car pull up outside and took a sharp intake of breath, snatching my keys and bag up off the sideboard, ushering Jack to hurry up, and heading out the door as ready as I would ever be.

"You look gorgeous, Louise, relax. Do you know where we are going yeh?" Jack said as he got in the taxi.

"Yeh, I've just given it to the driver, so we should be able to find it quite easily." We headed off onto the motorway in the direction that was shown. Kieran lived in a remote suburban village about an hour away from mine and I had heard that he had ploughed a huge deposit into this as it was his dream home. He was finally a firefighter, and his wife Sierra was a marketing director for a huge cosmetics firm based in London. I had gathered from his messages that she was the more dominant figure in the relationship and knew that this would suit him down to the ground.

After a few miles, we came off and directed down an unmarked lane. There were potholes filled with puddles causing the car to rock, bouncing us both back and forth. The driver turned his lights on full beam, and we could see the shadow of a house emerging. "I think this is it," I declared, turning to face Jack. The taxi stopped outside a small, pretty brick cottage. It had dazzling, sweet pink rosebushes dotted around the front garden behind a white picket fence, and a bright red front door with a shiny black door knocker placed in the centre. I looked around and noticed how picture-perfect the house was, as if it could be hiding many secrets behind this impeccable exterior. "Come on, you ready?" I looked at Jack.

"As I will ever be," he replied, undoing his seatbelt then leaning over to open the door. I took another deep breath and climbed out, giving the driver cash as I got out, thanking him, wondering if he had any clue as to what we were about to do.

"Go on, you press it," I laughed as we stood outside the front door.

"Jeez, you do it. They're your friends," Jack replied.

"OK, OK." I firmly pressed the doorbell and waited.

Kieran opened the door and welcomed me with a huge smile. He bent down to give me a hug that seemed to last forever, like he had genuinely missed my company. "How have you been?" he said, ushering us both inside.

"Yeh great thanks, so good to see you, and the house." I took a look around. The house was tidy but felt empty, not lived in yet. I knew that they had just recently moved in and I guessed they hadn't put their own stamp on the place. It was such a beautiful location that I was sure they had grand plans.

"Do you want a drink or anything?" Kieran asked, nodding in the direction of a bottle of wine on the coffee table next to some glasses.

"Why not, eh, fill her up," Jack declared, trying to break the ice.

Kieran poured the drinks and handed me one. Jack put a protective arm around my shoulder, sliding his hand down to my bum, stopping as he squeezed it, winking at me. My tummy was in knots.

Kieran edged closer in and started chatting to us both. He deliberately reached up to my hair and brushed it away from my face, leaning in, kissing me full on the lips. I was taken aback as Jack was standing right there next to me, and it felt odd, my instinct telling me that this was wrong. Jack pulled in closer toward me and pushed my body against Kieran's as a sign to say go on. The whole thing was out of the ordinary and I just didn't know how to handle myself.

I stood there like a piece of wood, stiff and unnatural. Thankfully, Sierra appeared from the room next door. Kieran spun around and grabbed her a drink. "Sierra, meet Louise and Jack. Louise, Jack, meet my beautiful wife Sierra."

"Hey," Jack and I said in a chorus together, slightly nervous, and raised our glasses as if to toast the night ahead.

"Well, lovely to meet you both. I have heard so much about you, Louise," Sierra said as she seemingly floated toward me in a cool, calm, and collected manner. She was wearing a tight-fitting blue cocktail dress, had her hair up in a chignon, and a full face of makeup on. She looked like she was the boss, like she knew what she was doing! I felt like an amateur next to her; she was beautiful.

As the night went on, we became more comfortable and chatted and laughed, drinking our fears away. They were a lovely couple, and I was in awe of how relaxed Sierra seemed in this situation. They had clearly done this hundreds of times before.

After numerous glasses of prosecco, Kieran made the first move. He edged closer to me, cupping my bum, took the glass from my hand, and placed it on the coffee table, pressing my body close to his. Again, he did his signature move and brushed my hair away from my face, lifting my face toward his, and kissed me slowly, darting his tongue inside my lips, parting them as he did so. I felt awkward, unsure as to what Jack would be feeling and thinking, knowing I wasn't too into Kieran. I tried to enjoy it as much as I could.

From the corner of my eye, I could see Sierra move toward us. She came up behind me and cupped my breasts, gently kissing my neck as Kieran moved his hands toward my knickers, placing his hand in and up through one of the slits in my dress. I could hear Jack murmuring behind us and hoped he was enjoying watching.

Kieran slowly placed a finger on top of my clit, rubbing it through the material on my knickers as I smiled. He watched my face intently. I turned to look at Jack, who was smiling at us and swigging at his drink. He gave me a wink as if to encourage me to carry on.

I moved my head back and kissed Sierra, enjoying feeling her tongue inside my mouth and Kieran touching my clit, rubbing gently and slowly, ensuring that I was comfortable.

Suddenly, Kieran pulled us apart and got down on his knees. He lifted my dress and pulled at my knickers, tugging them down to my ankles. Smiling up at me, he started kissing my clit and licked his fingers, slowly carefully inserting one inside me at a time. I couldn't help but get turned on. Sierra moved back and stood next to Jack, pouring herself another drink, watching our every move. I could feel her eyes on me at all times.

Enjoying the feeling of Kieran's hot breath on me, I steadied myself and spread my legs open further so that he could get his fingers deeper inside me. Knowing that he wanted me and had done for many years was turning me on. Feeling like

I was the one in control, I pulled his head back up, took my dress off, flung it to the side of the room, and stood there in my underwear and heels, letting him take in every inch of me.

I unbuttoned his shirt, feeling his huge pecs as they became exposed, and placing my hand around his muscular biceps, loving the size of his arms and his manly body. I dared to unbutton his jeans, pulling them down to his ankles so I could see his hard penis beneath his boxer shorts, smiling to myself, knowing how much he had wanted this moment. I looked around again at Jack and Sierra, who were intently watching us.

I took Kieran's erect penis out from under his boxer shorts and pulled up and down slowly, staring at the expression on his face. He looked happy, and I could tell he wanted more. He reached to cup my breasts, taking his other hand and fingering me urgently, moaning and groaning with every stroke enticing me closer toward his body. He kissed the top of my head and asked if I wanted him inside me yet.

I looked over at Jack and he nodded with his approval, edging in closer toward Sierra. I guess he was hoping he would get some action from her too.

I slowly slid my knickers down, leaving my heels on, and kicked the knickers to the side of the room. Sierra suddenly came up behind me and kissed my neck once more as Kieran continued to pump at my vagina with his fingers, staring at my face. Sierra carefully unhooked my bra from the back, exposing my breasts and nipples that were already getting hard with how turned on I was. I let out a sigh as I was fully immersed in the situation now and needed one of them inside me as my breath became more urgent.

I stepped back, carefully so as not to knock into Sierra, and walked toward the sofa, grabbing at Kieran's hand, smiling so that he knew what was coming. Kieran turned me around and asked me to bend over as he slid a condom onto his erect penis. I stood firmly in my heels and spread my legs, holding myself up onto the sofa cushions and looking back over my shoulder at the others.

Jack watched as I was bent over, and Kieran asked if I was happy as he placed himself inside me.

"Yes, go on," I uttered.

I turned my head to look back further and check that Jack was OK. His eyes met with mine and by the glint within them I could tell that he was more than OK—in fact, he looked like he was already enjoying it.

Kieran pushed further and further, deep inside my pussy. I let out a yelp as Sierra came over and gently caressed my left breast, leaning in to kiss my face. I looked up and tenderly kissed her full cherry-red lips, enjoying her softness and, feeling the warmth of her tongue inside my mouth, I could feel myself getting further turned on.

I could see Jack from the corner of my eye, leaning in nearer and nearer, until he got up and came closer to us. Kieran suddenly slowed down. We both looked at Jack as he leaned in and touched my clit, rubbing it softly and kissing my neck as Sierra continued to kiss my lips. He pushed Kieran back onto me and urged him to carry on, all whilst stroking my clit. I could see from the bulge in his jeans that he was enjoying this. I could tell he wanted to watch, enjoying seeing me have some fun. I just loved the way he thought, the way he was so open to new things, never judging, never questioning. Just taking people at face value.

Kieran continued to slowly pump at me, moaning and grunting as he did so. All I could think about was Jack—I wanted him too. I moved off Kieran and stood up, leaning over to unzip Jack's jeans and place his huge, throbbing cock in my hand. He was warm and his skin was soft and plump. I bent back over and motioned for Kieran to place himself inside of me once more, all whilst holding onto Jack, my hand moving firmly up and down his penis. Kieran thrust himself inside me deeper and I hovered over Jack's magnificent penis, looked up into his eyes, and winked. He smiled. I took that as a firm yes and placed him in my mouth, sucking and moving my lips around the tip whilst Kieran fucked me deeper, harder, and harder. I looked up and saw them high-five each other above me and smirked. Jack was enjoying this more than I had realised.

Sierra was sitting to the side of me on the sofa, and by this time just in her underwear, staring at us, touching her breasts, clearly getting turned on too. She saw me watching her and reached around, softly, touching my clit just as Kieran pushed one last time and I came. I screamed with delight, careful not to hurt Jack as he was still just inside my mouth.

Kieran pulled himself out of me and sat down next to Sierra. She got up and straddled him, my juices mixing with hers dripping over his balls. His eyes lit up as her magnificent, huge breasts bounced up and down above him. He quickly got hard again, and I could see her place him inside her as she ripped the condom off him, smirking all the way. I turned to look at Jack; he was watching them intently. "Faster," he whispered to me, and pushed my head down onto his penis.

I soon climbed on top of Jack, who was by this point on the floor, and placed his bare cock inside of me. We were both watching Kieran and Sierra. Kieran had moved Sierra over and was beating deep into her from behind whilst she moaned and groaned with pleasure, watching us from under her hair, giving us a smile every now and then.

Kieran soon let out a huge moan as he came inside her and practically pushed her away from him immediately. I could see that his juices were already dripping down her sleek, pale thighs.

Jack looked down at me and moved my head up toward his. He leaned down to kiss me, and I could feel him pulsating inside of me. I knew he was about to come so I carefully stepped off, still in my heels, and placed him back in my mouth, sucking long and hard, gulping down the copious amounts of cum that he ejected, sucking him until it was dry. Jack smiled at me and shivered. "Amazing, babe, you are so naughty."

"All for you babes," I said, reaching around to get my bra that had been tossed away.

Kieran and Sierra were both in their underwear, lounging on the sofa together, holding each other in an intimate embrace, both smiling but staring at us.

Jack looked over at them. "Well, that was interesting," he chuckled.

"For sure! I enjoyed that and hoped you both did too?" Kieran asked confidently.

"We certainly did!" Jack replied eagerly. "I guess we should get going now though," he stated as he grabbed his clothes and started to get dressed. "I would love to do it again sometime." He winked at me.

"Definitely," I quickly answered, not holding back.

I found my dress and tugged it over my head, pleased that he had enjoyed something new with me, but somehow, I felt anxious, wondering what he would want from me next. Where could we go from here? How naughty would he want to go next time? I wasn't sure how far I could go, but I knew I wasn't prepared to let him go without trying.

We both got dressed and politely thanked Kieran and Sierra for their time and agreed to do it again sometime soon and called ourselves a taxi.

Throughout the journey home, we both sat in silence. Jack appeared to be satisfied just staring out the window chilling, whilst my mind was running with thoughts of what would happen next, what did he think of me, and would he go and do something like that without me there? I felt anxious, insecure, and unworthy. It was definitely something different but not something I had ever thought of doing before.

"You OK, babe?"

"Yeh, why?"

"I don't know. You seem quiet. Was the night what you had expected?"

"Yeh, it was more than I could have expected. I loved it."

"That's good. I love making you happy, you know that don't you?"

"Ha, of course, you try hard to please me."

"Good, I'm glad you can appreciate my efforts. I want to be with you, properly with you, you know that right?"

"Babe, I don't want to hurt you. I don't know what I want. I enjoy having fun with you. That's enough, isn't it?"

I looked at Jack and smiled. There was no more that I could say. No other way that I could convey to him that I wanted to be his girlfriend, full time. I had explained my feelings clearly, but I still had no clue how he really felt about me. I wasn't sure if I was pushing the subject too much or if I was being insecure, so I didn't press it further. Once we reached my house, I invited him in for the night.

"Yeh, that would be good." Jack got out and followed me.

I was confused—we were hanging out more than ever, doing things that couples do together, but I felt that it was always on his terms. I pushed the thought to the back of my mind and drifted off into a deep sleep in his arms.

I woke up, stretched out, and looked at the clock; it was 7 a.m. I couldn't see Jack beside me. I got up and searched the house for him, but couldn't find him anywhere. I realised he had already left. No note, no text, nothing. My heart sank. He was playing with my emotions again. Did he not have any ounce of respect for me? I was gutted.

19

I sat on my sofa most of the day, flicking through Netflix mindlessly, watching the TV, trying to get my mind off of Jack. I felt let down and just wanted to know what was going on in his head.

It got to a point where I was fed up with wondering where I stood with Jack. He was constantly hot and cold, and I kept trying to figure out what I had done wrong. Should I just leave it and try to meet someone else, leave him in the past? Or was this just how he acted when he was in a relationship, casual and nonchalant? It certainly wasn't how I wanted our relationship to be. I wanted to see him all the time and speak to him every day, be able to depend on him if I needed to.

I resolved that another night out with Felicity would sort my low mood out. I wouldn't text Jack—I couldn't after our chat last night; it would appear needy, and I didn't want to push him away. I had to play it cool, act as if I was chilled or I was sure that he would lose interest.

"Hey chick, how are things? Fancy going out tonight?" I texted Felicity. Immediately I got a response back.

"Yes, I was just about to message you the exact same question. Great minds think alike!"

"Ah fab, shall I swing by in a taxi on the way into town and we can go to a bar for a catch up yeh?" I suggested.

"Sounds great to me, around 8pm?"

"Perfect."

I decided I was going to try to forget about Jack and concentrate on my life. Maybe Felicity and I should book a holiday to get away from things for a bit. Some sun, sea, and sand might just do the trick! What is it everyone says? A change of scenery does wonders, I think. I looked at my watch and realised I had three hours to get some food and get dressed for a night out.

I went upstairs and went through my wardrobe, deciding what I should wear. I stood there wondering if I should go dressed up or casual and eventually settled on a coral vest top with a light blue denim miniskirt. Dressing up would instantly make me feel better, I was sure. I laid out the clothes, accessories, and underwear and went back downstairs to see what I had in the fridge to line my stomach.

"Hey chick, you look nice," Felicity said as she got into the taxi.

"Thanks, babe, so do you." I smiled. "So, shall we go to the bar on the corner, you know, the quiet one, so we can catch up first then head on down to the club once we are suitably pissed?" I nudged her arm.

"Why not eh, you get the taxi fare, and I will get the first round in."

"Deal."

20

From the corner of my eye, I could see a figure that looked exactly like Jack. I turned around so I could get a better view and saw it was him, standing next to Steve and a petite, pretty, blonde-haired girl. Jack was leaning into her as if hanging onto her every word, spilling his drink as he moved in.

"Look who's over there!" I shouted to Felicity, motioning toward Jack.

"Oh, babe, I don't want any trouble tonight. Just leave him to it," she suggested as she gulped a mouthful of beer.

"I know, I know. It hurts, that's all," I replied and turned away.

Next thing I knew, Jack was on the dance floor standing right in front of me, dancing next to the girl. I couldn't work out if he had spotted me, but he was clearly extremely drunk.

Infuriated, I turned around and looked for the nearest half-decent man and started flirting, desperately trying to get Jack jealous. The guy gave me a cheeky smile and started grinding up close to my body. Although he wasn't bad looking, I had my eye firmly on what Jack was doing. The guy leaned in close and tried to kiss me. I swerved and smiled. It was totally immature behaviour on my part, but I wanted Jack to notice me, not to meet anyone new! He seemed oblivious to anyone else in the club. The night went on and the more I drank the more making him jealous became a good idea.

"What are you doing?" I felt Felicity's hand on my shoulder, pulling me off the guy. "Louise, Jack is watching you," she whispered into my ear.

"So, why should I care?" I answered, pulling myself back and edging toward the other bloke. At this point he must have sensed something was up and asked me if I had a boyfriend.

"Yeh, he's over there!" Felicity declared. I could feel the eyes of the club turn onto me. I knew I was acting ridiculous, but I did not care. I just wanted to hurt Jack like he had hurt me. The guy looked at me, then at Jack. He put his hands up in the air as if to surrender and walked away.

"He's not my boyfriend, Flic," I said.

"Well, I know you want him to be, so act like it!"

She was right. If I kept behaving the way I was going, I was never going to give it a good enough go.

"Oh look, there's Nicole." Felicity pointed toward a group in the corner of the room. I could vaguely make out a silhouette and saw Nicole dancing in the middle of the group whilst everyone around her was watching. She had always been gorgeous; her petite frame with beautiful, shiny brown hair made her stand out from the crowd and she had a cheeky sense of humour.

"Cool, let's go over and see how she is!" I declared, stumbling toward the group with one eye still firmly on Jack.

"Hey." I went over to Nicole and clinked glasses with her. "How's tricks? With Liam tonight, are you?"

"He's over there with Jack and Steve." Nicole pointed toward the dance floor. The three boys were laughing, joking, and having a dance. The pretty blonde girl was still standing next to Jack.

"Ah OK, they look cosy, don't they?" I blurted out.

"They do, don't they, who is she?" Nicole also questioned.

"No idea," I stated, scoffing my drink down to block out any feelings of jealousy that could potentially rear up.

"Why don't we go over?"

"Ah girls, come on, I really am not in the mood for drama tonight," Felicity declared. Nicole and I just looked at each other, smiled, and walked over toward the boys.

"Hey!" I went straight over to Jack, making myself known. Jack stumbled backwards, spilling his drink. He looked me up and down. "Hey, you OK?" he asked, clearly drunk and unsure as to what he should say to me.

"Come here, gorgeous, give me a kiss," I demanded, claiming my man in front of the blonde.

"I've just got to pop to the loo, back in a sec," he declared, and off he went, drink in hand.

"Hmm, something's not right here," I whispered in Felicity's ear.

"Can we just have a good night, no drama or fighting, yeh?" she replied. I took that as I was being overdramatic and tried to calm myself down.

"Yeh, let's get another drink." I pulled Felicity over to the bar and ordered another drink for us both. Nicole was standing with Liam, and they looked engrossed in a serious conversation.

Drink in hand, Felicity and I went back onto the dance floor and danced away, making up silly dances and laughing at who could dance the worst between ourselves. She had me in stitches, pulling the funniest of faces, open-mouthed and screeching the words to the songs out loud. I was having such fun I hadn't noticed that Jack had slipped out of the club without saying goodbye. At nearly closing time, Nicole came over to us and joined in. We were all dancing and chatting away when all of a sudden Liam came over and kissed Nicole on the cheek goodbye.

"Where's he off to in a hurry?" I asked, curious as to where the blonde, Jack, and Steve had got to.

"Oh, he's going back to Steve's now, I think. Jack's already left, if that is what you were wondering."

"Hmm, yeh, nice of him to say goodbye to me. He's just so hot and cold!" I shouted.

"He's weird with you. Leave him be," Felicity said. "He can't be that into you if he is treating you like this so early on.

Surely at this stage you are meant to be on your best behaviour. No??"

"Ah I know, Flic, but when we are alone it's magical. He's attentive, sweet, caring, the list goes on."

"Pass me the sick bucket," Nicole interrupted, mimicking being sick by gently placing two fingers near her mouth and retching. "Either try to forget him or confront him head-on babes!"

"I know, I know, he just gets under my skin. I'm literally like putty in his hands and every ounce of bravado disappears when I'm with him. I find it hard to get the right words out when we are alone as it all seems perfect when he's there. I don't want to spoil that moment by bringing up things that have happened in the past."

"Why don't you both come back to mine? Let's not let the night end now!" Nicole nudged my arm as if to get me back into the present moment and enjoy the evening.

"You're on," I stated, glad that I wouldn't be going home alone.

"Ah, I'm OK, girls, I'm going to get a taxi."

"OK, let's all jump in together and you get dropped off first, then we can go onto Nicole's house. Yeh?"

"Fab, I'll call one now," Felicity replied, taking her phone out of her bag and dialling the number. Within five minutes we were all piling into the taxi, laughing and joking, trying to hold our coats and bags as we scrambled for the seatbelts. Soon enough Felicity had been dropped off and we were at Nicole's house.

"Here, have this." Nicole handed me a vodka.

"Cheers," I toasted her glass, simply happy to be continuing the night. "What's all this?" I asked, pointing to a pile of unused SIM cards resting on the edge of her sofa.

"My friend Olivia gave me a load; she works in the phone shop down the high street. I think they are knocked off, but they do work! I was going to sell them on and try to make some money. Take it if you want, I have loads. It's a top-up only, so it won't cost you anything."

"Ah, OK, why not," I replied, putting one in my pocket, wondering how I could put it to good use.

"So tell me, what is going on with Liam then?" I asked. Nicole's eyes lit up as she began to unload her personal dating saga.

21

I had not heard from Jack for over a month by now. I knew something had changed, even before I had seen him with the girl in the club. I felt that he had taken me for granted and was using me just for sex. It was either that or I was getting paranoid because I had started to get strong feelings for him.

The weeks turned into months and eventually I stopped waiting for him. I knew he had moved on once again. He was always going to hold such a special place in my heart, but I couldn't just sit and wait for him. As far as I was concerned, I was five years older than him, already approaching my late twenties, and I wanted to start to look at settling down with someone who could provide me with love and stability. If Jack was not ready for this, then so be it.

Often, I thought of him, and it just made me angry. I felt like I had given my all to him, sold my soul to the devil, and he just didn't seem to care. I wanted to get back at him, make him notice me and for him to realise he couldn't play me like he had done.

I thought for a while, and I realised exactly how to get back at him. After Nicole had given me the extra SIM card, I knew I could set up an account and prank him through texts. I thought about what to type all day, trying to figure out how best to get at him.

"Hi, it's Kate. It was great to meet you Saturday night. Fancy meeting up for a drink this week?" I typed out, knowing he would have gone out at some point over the weekend and given his number to some random girl.

"Oh Hi, I was really drunk this weekend, sorry for my behaviour. It would be lovely to meet up."

He fell for it! I couldn't quite believe it was true—although I felt smug getting back at him, my heart sank that he was already meeting other girls.

"Ha ha, you were fine! I was drinking a lot too to be honest. OK, how about outside the train station in town, say 8pm Thursday night? We can see where the night takes us?" I replied, trying to take the conversation onto a slightly risqué stance, hoping he would fall for it and assume I was some gorgeous chick he had met out at the weekend and given his number to. Clearly, he had no idea who it was and was so out of it he had assumed it was real.

The week went past slowly. I had a lot of meetings at work and John was keeping me busy. I had managed to get out to the gym on a couple of lunch breaks, but there was nothing exciting going on.

Eventually Thursday evening arrived. I had butterflies in my tummy knowing I was being out of order pranking Jack like this, but I couldn't help it. I wanted to hurt him like he had me, and it was the only way I could think of to get the upper hand.

At 8 p.m. on the dot I sat at home on my sofa with the new SIM card in my phone and a cup of fresh herbal tea in my hand, waiting for his text.

"Where are you? I'm here," he typed at exactly 8.05 p.m.

"I can see you. I'm in a red jumper, over by the main entrance," I lied.

"I can't see you. Where are you?" he replied.

I sat there laughing, knowing full well this was ridiculous behaviour and also very cruel. I instantly felt better, though—he had played games with me, and I felt like I had gotten back at him. I just wanted to be on top and to show him who the boss was after he had made me feel so low.

"Over by the entrance," I continued. Suddenly the phone

rang. I had no idea what to do. I couldn't answer it as he would know my voice. I just let it go to voicemail and hoped for the best.

"Can't you see me?" I proceeded, laughing as I typed.

"No, is this a set up?"

"Of course not," I lied again.

"Well, if you don't show in 5 minutes I'm going home," Jack typed. I almost felt sorry for him.

"Ha ha sucker!" I typed, knowing I couldn't take it any further. I wanted him to know it was me who set him up.

"Who is this?" he asked.

"Who do you think?"

"Quit the games and just tell me."

"Louise!"

"Oh hi, how are you? I'm just on my way home now."

Damn, I was not expecting that reply. He had stumped me. Of course, he had said he was on his way home though, non-committal and aware that I would try to meet up with him whilst he was in town.

"Sorry, it was too easy to get you to fall for it!" I admitted, knowing full well this was probably the last time I would speak to him and that this was a serious step too far.

"Not funny Louise!" he replied. *"Catch up soon."* And with that I knew he was going to stop the conversation. Like so many times before, it would be on his terms. He was the boss in this relationship, or whatever it actually was. I was completely subservient to his every need. I put the phone away in a drawer in the bedroom and tried to forget about it. I knew it was a horrible way to trick someone, but I had also wanted that contact with him. Pretending to be someone else gave me the disguise that I needed in order to speak with him again. It had of course backfired. In all honesty, what had I really expected to happen?

I sat on my bed, sobbing. I felt like I had lost him. I knew he wasn't interested anymore, and I wanted either closure or to see him again to try to ignite those feelings and connection we shared. I tried to think of a way we could meet up, or even subtly bump into each other, but I had exhausted every possible avenue I could think of.

I was truly besotted, and I knew I had to get a grip on my emotions before I lost all sense of who I really was. Sometimes I wished I hadn't met him at all. The pain of wanting and needing to see him all the time and wondering if he still cared was driving me bonkers.

22

"Hey, what have you been up to?"

I couldn't help it, I had caved in and texted him. I just wanted to see him, although I had left it a month before texting him, hoping he would calm down enough for us to start talking again.

"*Hey! Nothing much, busy with work, you?*" he replied as if nothing had ever gone wrong.

"*Yeh, work's been busy for me too. Fancy meeting up soon. I'd love to see you!*" I eagerly replied before I chickened out of asking him to meet up.

"*OK, how about tomorrow at the café on the layby near town. At 8pm?*"

My heart skipped a beat—he wanted to meet up! "*Sounds great. See you then,*" I replied. I couldn't contain my excitement. Finally, I was getting to see him again! I put my phone down on the coffee table and started planning which outfit I would wear in my head, mindlessly flicking through the channels on the TV and not actually taking any of it in.

The following evening came around and I had decided on dressing fairly casual in trainers, loose light blue jeans, and a tight white vest top. I had completely plucked and preened myself, ensuring I was smooth and ready to get naked with him should we go back to his.

I pulled into the layby. There were no other cars parked, but I hopefully texted him to see if he was coming. "*Where are you? I'm here,*" deep down knowing full well I had been stood up.

"*At home,*" came the reply. At least he was honest, I guess.
"*Ha ha very funny. Why won't you meet up?*" I asked. No reply.
I tried calling. No answer. That was it, things had definitely taken a turn for the worse and become toxic. I knew I was partly to blame. I turned my car engine on and drove home feeling utterly deflated.

I was still so desperate to hear from Jack, but nothing came of it and once again I tried to push him to the back of my mind. It was hard because something kept pulling me back. Deep down I felt that we were meant to be together, and that he was also thinking of me. Wishful thinking? I wasn't quite sure, but the feelings I had were real enough to me no matter how hard I tried to suppress them.

23

The next eight months flew by quickly, and I had still not heard from Jack. I knew that the fake messages and hurtful things that had gone on between us meant it was over. I often thought of Jack and our time together, wishing things could have been different.

One hot, balmy summer evening I was outside the front of my house, chatting to my neighbour. I heard a loud roar of a motorbike heading down the road, coming toward us. We both looked up and watched as the man on the bike stormed past us, revving the engine loudly. There was something about the figure on the bike, something familiar, and it made my heart skip a beat. It was Jack, I just knew it!

My gaze followed the bike, and I could see it go off around the bend and pull over at a nearby house. I was intrigued and edged forward from my driveway, watching like a crazed person. I saw the rider get off the bike, grabbing at his helmet and pulling it off. It was Jack! I knew it! He pulled some keys out of his pocket and headed into the house. My head was thumping; even seeing him made me want him. I knew I was still not over him.

I decided to wave just in case he was looking and then went back inside my house with my thoughts racing. What was he doing there? Why did he have keys—was he living near me now? If so, why hadn't he tried to contact me? My heart sank. He always seemed to pop back into my life, and I found it so hard not to think of him and of what could have been between us.

I immediately phoned Felicity. "Can you believe it, Flic, I mean of all the places that he could live! Why hasn't he called me?"

"Oh, Louise, I don't know, maybe he has moved on, maybe he wants to leave that chapter of his life behind? Try not to dwell on it. It's not good for you."

"I know, I just can't stop wanting him. Those feelings don't just disappear. I was in love with him."

"Well, unless he contacts you, you have to just forget him and try as hard as you can to move on."

"Yeh, you're right. Fancy coming over to watch a movie or something soon, yeh?"

"Sounds fab, Friday night?"

"8 p.m. and it's a date, my gorgeous!" With that I put the phone down, content that I now had plans for the weekend and feeling better to have aired my thoughts to my best friend.

Friday night ended up being extremely tame for Felicity and me. I didn't mention Jack, and Felicity told me all about her most recent date and the fact that she had seen him a couple of times since then. It sounded like it was going well, and I was really happy for her.

I saw Jack out several times over the next few months. He was always with a beautiful, petite, blonde girl, and mostly holding her hand like she was a prized possession. I'd caught him staring at her lovingly once and it was heartbreaking to watch, but as he was no longer in my life, I just had to get him out of my head and keep working on getting over him. He hadn't ever acknowledged me or even noticed me.

One night I bumped into Steve while I was having a drink and he told me that Jack was living with his new girlfriend at the house near mine. I wondered if it was as awkward for him as it was for me.

24

Months passed and I hadn't seen Jack. I was always looking out for his motorbike, hoping to even just catch a glimpse of him, but it never happened again.

Almost a year later I was out shopping in town when I physically bumped into him. I was walking up the high street and the sun was shining brightly in my line of vision. I tried to block it out with my hand and was edging close to the shop doorways so as not to be pushed off into the road, and, bam, suddenly I ran into someone. I stepped further into the doorway of a shop and heard the familiar voice. "Are you OK? So sorry I didn't see you there." I felt an arm grab me.

"That's OK, I couldn't see very well because of the sun," I replied, wondering where I had heard that voice before. "Oh, Jack!" I exclaimed as he turned me around and stood in front of me, out of the sun.

"Hey, you, how's tricks?" He smiled at me.

"Yeh, all good, thanks. How are you? What's new?" I could feel myself wanting to straighten my hair and clothes out, wishing I had worn a different, more flattering outfit that day.

"Not much, you know, working, working, working!" He chuckled. "You're looking well. Who are you seeing now?"

I gulped, embarrassed that I was still single. "No one, still carefree and single!" I admitted.

"Well, that's good. Me too. You know, I really don't know what happened between us. Would you like to go out sometime?"

"Jack, come on, we've been here before. We always seem to mess each other up in some way. Our track record is not great."

"Ah, yeh, but I've grown now. I still miss you." He winked.

I wanted nothing more than to see him, be with him, and have mind-blowing sex with him again and again. But I knew it was not good for me to go back down that road. "Well, I have the same number as always, so give me a call." I smiled, turned on my heel, and walked off, biting my lip, hoping that he still knew my number.

"Wait." Jack tugged at my arm. "I don't have it any longer. I've changed phones since then. Come on, what is it?" he said, passing me his phone to type the digits into. I looked up at him and sighed, bashing my number in, double-checking it was correct before giving it back.

"Here you go then. Jack, if you want me, you come and get me," I said and turned away once more, blowing him a kiss and a wink as I did so. I knew he loved my cheekiness, and I wanted to show him that this time, he needed to work hard to get me.

That evening I phoned Felicity to tell her what had happened.

"You didn't give him your number though, did you?" she said, "You're both so toxic together, it's not a good idea."

"I did! And I'm pleased that I did. I've not stopped thinking about him, Felicity. You know he turns my head like no other."

"He has a hold of you and I've no idea why. Just be careful is all I will say." Felicity sighed. "Anyway, what are you doing at the weekend? Shall we go up to London, something different?"

"I'd love it! Why not? Saturday night, yeh?"

"Yeh, same time. Meet at mine, and we can get the train together. It looks like it might be sunny too. We could get a bite to eat beforehand."

"Flic, I've gotta go. I've just heard a text come through and

I want to see if it's Jack. I'll keep you posted, but Saturday is on."

"OK, speak soon."

"Hey! It was so good to see you earlier. You are looking hot! Did you have a good shopping trip today?" It was from Jack.

"BINGO," I shouted, thrilled that he was already messaging me. I knew I had to play this right. I knew that I had to at least try to act demure and wait for a while before jumping into replying. "Make him wait, sweat it out," I said to myself.

An hour later I decided it was OK to reply. Besides, I wanted to chat with him too! *"Hey, yeh very random, eh? I bought a few good bits yeh. How about you?"*

"What are you up to? Fancy meeting up?" he replied within a nanosecond. He was such a strange character, either full-on or totally dismissive. I never quite knew where I stood with him. I guessed that was his charm but wondered where this was going.

"Can't tonight, fancy tomorrow?" I replied, trying to maintain a bit of mystery and some control.

"Yeh OK. Why don't you come to mine, we can catch up over a drink and you can tell me what you have been up to? My housemate will be out, so it will just be us."

"OK, send me your address and I'll pop over. Is 8pm good?"

"Perfect," Jack replied with his address and a wink emoji.

Great, it was a date. I wondered if I had opened Pandora's box by reuniting those feelings again.

The next day at work I couldn't tell Karen what I was up to. I knew she would say the same thing that Felicity had. I was nervous, not for meeting him or being with him, but for any after effects that could happen. I kept my head down and got stuck into work. Luckily it was a busy day and John was in the office demanding things were done instantly.

That evening I couldn't eat because my nerves were on fire. I decided on some soup and wondered if I was doing the right thing as I ate, pondering the various scenarios that could happen after seeing him.

I had decided on going casual. I took out my loose-fitting light blue jeans and a simple tight pink T-shirt with some new bright white underwear underneath. At least I would feel sexy under all the casual gear. I slowly straightened my hair, put some shine serum on it, then plastered my makeup meticulously, ensuring my lips were looking full and my eyelashes curled to perfection.

There. As ready as I'll ever be, I thought to myself, looking in the full-length mirror by the front door. I knew I looked extremely informal and laid back, but underneath I was seriously nervous, my palms sweaty and my heart already racing. I gathered my bag and locked my front door.

Typing the address into the sat nav, I noted that it was only twenty minutes away, but toward another nearby town that I didn't know too well. I couldn't help checking my hair and makeup in the rearview mirror at every traffic light, checking I did not have lipstick on my teeth and fluffing up my cheeks. I eventually turned down his road and looked around at the houses. It was a new development of small houses and a couple of terraces. I looked down at my phone for the number; he was at Number 20, which was the detached family-looking home, tucked furthest in the corner. I parked on the driveway and got out, butterflies in my stomach.

"Hey! Come in," Jack exclaimed as he opened the door before I even rang the bell.

"Great, all the better for seeing you," I replied as he ushered me inside, leaning in to give me that all-so-familiar kiss on the cheek. "What would you like to drink?"

"Surprise me!" I offered, feeling brave as I sat on the sofa, taking in the new surroundings. It was a large open-plan living room, neutrally decorated in magnolia. I wondered who he was living with this time and what the story was behind it.

"So, who are you sharing with?" I asked.

"A guy from work. I moved out from living with my ex, it's nearer to my office here too. He has his girlfriend over a lot though," Jack said as he rolled his eyes, passing me a hot cup of tea.

"Thanks, I don't drink tea much. I find the caffeine affects me," I said, taking a sip anyway. "Is that the ex-girlfriend who lives near me?"

"How do you know?" he asked.

"I saw you with her on your motorbike a few times. Looking sexy as ever, I might add." I winked.

"Haha, I like it. Go on, sit down, tell me what you have been up to. I'm intrigued."

I sat down next to him on the edge of the cream leather sofa, but I was unable to relax. I couldn't work out what he wanted this time. It was obvious he wanted sex, that was always a given from Jack, but was that it, did he want to date me or just use me?

"Well, I still work for John. It's getting busier but not much else has changed. I've started a new course, whilst still working so that I can gain a new qualification in law and hopefully go up a pay level at work. It's all very dull to be honest. I've missed you, though," I declared.

"Me too," he replied, tenderly clasping my cheek and moving closer so that we could kiss. He softly brushed his lips against mine and I could feel the heat from his breath as his breathing got faster. Knowing how much his body wanted mine made me crave him immediately.

"That was nice," I replied, leaning nearer to his body.

Jack smiled at me, slowly moving his hand over my breast, cupping it and squeezing it, encouraging my nipples to go hard. I let out a sigh of relief, instinctively knowing what was going to happen between us.

He then moved his hand down to my stomach, undoing the top button and unzipping my jeans. He moved his hand down to my knickers and placed his fingers inside them. He looked up at me, anticipating and waiting for me to give him the OK. I tenderly moved his chin up and kissed his full, red lips, taking in his saliva. Jack gently pushed a finger inside me. Already wet and anticipating his next move, I felt myself become even more turned on.

I reached down to touch his hardened manhood and instantly unzipped his jeans, grabbing it while he continued to play with me. I could feel myself getting wetter and just wanted him inside me, to feel that oh-so-familiar connection we have together.

I bent down, moved his hands out of my knickers, and placed him inside my mouth, licking and sucking whilst he inhaled deeply, moaning with pleasure. It was turning me on too—I had to have him there and then. It had been so long since we'd been together. I quickly stood up and took my jeans and T-shirt off, moving around. I straddled him, my face breaking into a smile.

I pushed the crotch of my knickers to the side and grabbed his huge cock, carefully slipping it up inside my dripping pussy. Moving on top of him, riding him, feeling him inside of me like all the times before, I was in ecstasy.

Jack then pushed me off his lap and swung me around, bending me over so he could enter me from behind, pumping me deep and hard. I let out a scream—I remembered that feeling, like he was made for me, a perfect fit. Faster and faster we moved together. I came quickly, and he pulled out.

"Swallow," he demanded. I placed my lips around him, remembering how big he was, and gulped, loving the feeling of his warm semen in my mouth and listening to the noises he made as I did so.

"Well, I have certainly missed this!" I exclaimed after I had cleaned myself up and put my clothes back on.

"Me too babes, me too," Jack laughed, pulling his jeans back on and then grabbing at his T-shirt.

He switched the TV back on as I snuggled up into the crook of his arm, looking up at him adoringly, happy to be sat there with him once again.

We thoughtlessly flicked through the TV channels as we laughed and chatted about what we had both been up to since we last saw each other.

25

The next few weeks were extremely busy at work, and one evening it was hard to leave the stress behind. My thoughts were racing, and I was not concentrating on the road. I was driving fast and came up to a roundabout, misjudging the queue of traffic. I hadn't pressed the brake hard enough and my car skidded into the verge with a *bang*! It came to a halt against a mound of grass. I lunged forward, feeling the pressure of the seatbelt keeping me in. "Oh, shit!" I cried, annoyed that I had been so careless whilst driving, thinking I was in control on such a stormy night.

I reached for my phone and dialled the recovery company, quoting my reference number that I had stored under the contact number and shivering in the cold.

It wasn't long before they turned up. The driver of the tow truck stated that he thought my car might be a right off.

They pulled the car completely off the road and onto the back of the lorry and drove me home. I was given the name of the garage to call to discuss the damage.

At home, I tried to rest but I felt a failure. Such a simple turn of events that could have been avoided. I drank copious amounts of chamomile tea and tried to calm down, telling myself that I was lucky it wasn't worse and that I was healthy.

I went to the toilet, but as I pulled my knickers down, I saw a clot of blood staining my knickers. I knew immediately what it was. I had come off the pill again when I wasn't seeing Jack and I had been a few days late for my period, again unheard of for me, and this did not look like it was a normal period.

I just knew. It was certainly an incredibly early miscarriage. Without realising how upset, shocked, and worried I was, a tear slowly fell down my face. I hadn't realised how much I had wanted a baby until this moment. I think I had been in denial, putting it to the back of my mind.

I managed to clean myself up and flushed the remnants of the clot down the loo, trying not to look back as I went into the kitchen to make myself another cup of hot tea.

I sat down at the table and went through the photos from the crash on my phone.

I decided I needed to let my parents know what had happened and phoned them. Relaying the story back to them seemed to put things into perspective. These things happened and I was lucky not to be hurt.

I couldn't quite put the blood spotting to the back of my mind. I was sad that it had happened and wanted to know what Jack would have to say about it. I sent him a picture of my crumpled car, not even knowing how he would react to that. My phone rang immediately, and I answered to Jack's concerned voice. "Are you OK? What happened?"

I relayed the story to him and assured him that I was fine. I couldn't bring myself to tell him about the blood over the phone, so I didn't mention it. I had promised myself I would let him know when I saw him next.

The next evening, I came home from work to find a huge bunch of flowers outside the door. I opened the tiny card attached to the flowers and inside it read:

To my brave and beautiful Louise, thinking of you always, Jack. Xx

I smiled as I placed the flowers on my sideboard in the hallway and hunted for a vase to neatly arrange them in. How thoughtful of him; he could be a kind soul sometimes.

26

That weekend, I was chatting to Felicity on the phone and deciding when to next meet up.

"Let's go out tonight, just to The Velvet Room!"

"Oh, I'm not so sure, Flic, I feel like we have done the nightlife there so many times, there's never anything new to explore. It's just the same old people and the same old stuff."

"Go on, it will be good to catch up. It's not about where we go, but who we are with!"

"Oh, OK, go on, you have twisted my arm," I joked, hardly looking forward to the venue but wanting to see Felicity regardless.

Deciding what to wear was easy. I grabbed a slim-fitting mint green vest top, some tight-fitting dark blue jeans, and my dark green court shoes with beautiful rainbow effect sequins dotted on the front. They were extremely high-heeled but elongated my legs, so I justified the extra discomfort in order to look nice for the evening.

I called a taxi and downed a vodka, lime, and soda before leaving, ready to get myself in the mood and loosen up a bit as I had been so tense since the crash.

Picking Felicity up on the way, I wondered if I would see Jack out too. I had phoned him the next day to thank him for the beautiful flowers he had sent and asked when we were next going to meet up. He wouldn't commit to a date and said he would let me know as he had a lot on. It made me feel rejected and I could not tell him about the miscarriage as I knew that it was not something to tell him over the phone and to be honest, I wanted to see his reaction face to face.

"Right, here we are, ladies. That's ten pounds please," the taxi driver called out to us. I handed him the £10 note and opened the taxi door.

"Come on, Flic, let's get lively," I said to Felicity as I handed her our first drink.

"Haha, I wasn't expecting a full-on night out, just a catch-up. Slow down, you!" she exclaimed.

Out of the corner of my eye I could see a figure of a bloke that looked familiar. I looked over and realised it was Steve. He was wearing a tight white T-shirt—clearly he had been working out; his muscles were pumped, and he was showing his arms off for full effect.

"Oh, Louise, don't go over. Just forget about him tonight, yeh," Felicity urged as she followed my gaze.

"No, you're right, babes, I just wanted to come out with you, catch up and have a laugh. I won't go over." I smiled at her, moving around to the nearest table so that we could sit and chat.

An hour later Steve appeared at our table. "Evening, ladies."

"Hey, you OK?" I asked, looking behind him to see if Jack was with him.

"Yeh, all good here, you two? What's new?" he asked, sitting down next to me as I budged up toward Felicity on the soft velvet sofa enveloping our table. "Fancy a shot?" Steve asked, clearly already intoxicated.

"Yeh, go on," Felicity shouted. "Make mine a Jagerbomb."

"OK, times two, yeh. Coming right up." Steve got up and headed to the bar.

"Why did you say yes?" I asked, wondering why she would have invited him over knowing she didn't want any company.

"Well, he was going to stay anyway. We might as well make him useful." She sniggered.

"Yeh, I like your way of thinking. He seems wasted, doesn't he?"

"Utterly! It's hilarious!"

"We don't have to wait for him if you want to move away? He will probably forget where we are anyway."

"Na, you're alright. I can't be bothered to get up and move."

"OK, well don't blame me if he commandeers our whole evening," I warned just as Steve returned with a tray full of Jagerbomb shots for the three of us.

"Ready, 1, 2, 3," he counted, not waiting until we were ready and drinking his own. I followed suit, feeling the warm, sticky, sharp taste go down my throat and wincing. No matter how many times I did it, it still made me shiver. It wasn't pleasant but would certainly take the edge off.

Felicity and I looked at each other, winced, and giggled. "At least we got a free drink I suppose!" she whispered in my ear.

"Well, yeh, I guess that's one bonus," I replied, smiling at Steve. He was a sweet soul really. Handsome, trendy, and extremely popular, but there seemed to be so much more going on behind the front that he put on. That's how I always felt about him anyway. I had always liked Steve and assumed that he was a good friend of mine too but I knew his loyalties would always lie with Jack so I had to be wary of him and of what I said about Jack.

"Let's go and have a dance." Felicity grabbed at my arm. Smiling at Steve, I got up and went back onto the dance floor.

A few moments later, Steve was standing over us. "Come back to mine," he suggested. "We can have a good catch-up; it's been a while, Louise."

"Yeh, OK, why not!" I agreed, noticing how quiet the club was becoming as it drew closer to closing time. "Felicity, you coming?" I shouted in her direction.

"Na, you're alright. Not sure it's the best idea though, Louise, you sure?"

"Yeh, it's just a catch-up. What could possibly go wrong?"

"Loads!" she chuckled, downing her drink. "I'll get a cab from outside, you going now, yeh?" she questioned.

"Yeh, I think so, that's what you meant, Steve, wasn't it?"

"Of course, come on. It's nearly closing time anyway."

We made our way out of the club and there was a line of taxi cabs waiting. Felicity got into one and Steve and I in the other. Although he only lived a short walk away from the town centre, it was a smart move as my shoes were stifling my feet.

It felt weird to be sitting so close to Steve, alone in the taxi. I looked out the window and wished that Jack was the one sitting next to me.

"You OK?" Steve asked as I fiddled about with the contents of my bag.

"Yeh, fine," I lied.

"Here we are, mate. Pull over just in front of that red car just here," Steve urged the driver. We paid the fare and got out. Steve jangled his keys in his hand, swaying as he placed the correct one in the lock, clearly more intoxicated than I was.

"In you go, my lady," Steve laughed as he stepped aside and motioned with his hands for me to lead the way into his home.

"Why thank you, kind sir," I giggled, feeling like I was on a date and being shown the best version of himself.

I looked about the lounge as I had done so many times before and noticed how strange it felt without Jack. It was tidier than usual, but there was no doubt it was a bachelor pad. The room had no soul, no finesse; it was just a room with stuff and an open-plan kitchen to the back. It was a gorgeous, modern house that must cost a lot to rent each month. There was a large black leather corner sofa and a huge TV. There were wires in front that belonged to a PlayStation and empty coke cans left half-full on the glass coffee table. I walked to the sofa and sat down, taking my coat off and placing my bag on top.

"Would you like a drink? I can open some white wine if you like?" Steve offered, already grabbing a bottle from his fridge.

"Yeh, if you fancy some too! Thanks, buddy," I replied, feeling a little on edge for some reason.

"So, what have you been up to lately without your partner in crime then?" I initiated, wanting to get the conversation switched onto Jack.

"Ah you know, getting my life in order, meeting new people." He chuckled as he pulled the cork out of the bottle, swishing the cool liquid into two glasses.

"Met anyone special lately then?" I probed as Steve handed me a glass and sat down on the sofa next to me.

"There was this one girl, I'm not sure if you had seen me with her out and about at all but that's sadly finished. I can admit I'm absolutely gutted but she doesn't want anything more to do with me, so I've got to try to move on."

"Did she have long, dark hair? Quite petite?" I asked.

"Yes, that's her."

"It's so hard when relationships end, and you are not ready for the end, isn't it? I've felt like that a lot with Jack. I wonder how he is feeling after splitting with his girlfriend?" I probed as Steve moved in closer, resting his hand on the sofa next to my leg.

"You mean to say you don't know? They are still together, Louise!"

"You are kidding me, he's still with her?! I saw him not long ago and he told me they had split up!"

"Yes!" Steve replied. "He has been for ages. They had a few arguments, so he moved out, nearer to his work for convenience, but they never completely split up."

"Well, that must have been when he moved out then. I can't believe he would lie to me."

"Louise, come on, he's played you. He just wanted to have sex, one for the road, you know what he's like!" Steve placed his drink on the table and turned to face me, shocked that I hadn't realised any of this after all this time.

"I just don't believe it. For one thing, she is stunning, why would he cheat on her? For another thing, why did he lie to me, why aren't we together if he thinks of me and wants to be with me?" I blurted out. I was just sick of it all. "He plays with my emotions; he leads me on and makes me look a fool." I felt so angry with the way I had been treated, tossed aside, used, and abused. No apologies. No nothing.

"I, I...I..." Tears were already forming in my eyes, big, bulbous wet drops falling onto my cheeks. "No, it's not true. It can't be."

"Louise, it is. He's not the man you think he is, or even want him to be."

I got up, grabbed my coat and bag, and ran out of the room, trying to remember which way I had come in. Every turn looked the same and I felt like I was going around in circles, engulfed by the high, closed walls. I felt claustrophobic and needed some air. My breathing became rapid, and the tears were still falling. Eventually I found the door. I almost fell inside the doorway as I sat crouched in a ball, crying hysterically, knowing I could be heard but not caring as my sobs were uncontrollable.

"Louise, where are you going? Are you OK?" I could hear Steve shouting through the door, but I couldn't reply.

I felt like I had gone past the point of no return, and it was like a devastation had hit me like nothing I had felt before. I felt sick. I didn't want to be me anymore; I couldn't live with this situation any longer. Acknowledging that this was as far as I could go, I needed to move on from Jack, for sanity's sake if nothing else.

27

"Hey, how are you feeling today? Why don't you come over, we can have pizza and a proper catch up," Steve's text read the next evening. He clearly knew I was still feeling rubbish and he obviously needed some company too.

"OK, sounds fun," I typed back, placing my phone on the coffee table and getting up off the sofa. I went straight to my bedroom to pick out an outfit to wear. I decided to go casual and picked out a pair of tight black jeans and a pale pink loose-fitting crew-neck jumper. I took a quick shower to freshen up and put on some heels, grabbing my bag with my car keys as I ran out the door.

I pulled up beside his front door and found a secure parking space. I got out and pressed the buzzer to his house, taking a deep breath. I was feeling apprehensive but also curious as to what he had to say. I mean, we hadn't exactly been great friends before all this but I had genuinely liked him so it would be good to see what happened and to find out more about Jack so that I could feel fully informed and move on.

"Hey!" Steve ushered me in. "Come here and sit next to me." He walked back into the living room and sat down, patting the seat beside him for me to sit next to him.

I tentatively sat down and placed my bag on the table. I wondered where the night would go from here; it still felt very surreal sitting here next to one of Jack's best friends without him being here with me.

"So, how are you feeling now?" Steve asked.

"Well, all the better for getting some company!" I joked. "I'm still in shock and wondering how I could have been sucked in like that. I thought I was stronger than this, that's all. I do, er, did, really like him," I corrected myself.

"Louise, he's very manipulative, he's a clever guy. I would not trust him as far as I could throw him. There's so much I could tell you."

"Go on," I urged.

"You know that motorbike is mine, don't you? I lent it to him. I hear he's been going around saying that it was his."

"What?!"

"Yeh, he owes me a lot of money too. I have no idea if I will ever get it back."

"No, he specifically told me that the motorbike was his!"

"See, I thought so. I was the one who bought it and because I am hardly using it, I lent it to him. I walk to work from here so it sat outside mostly, and he asked if he could borrow it one day. I said yes, but then he kept on taking it while I wasn't here and, well, the rest is history. He really isn't a nice person, Louise. I'm sorry to be the one to tell you all this." Steve looked me straight in the eye and took my hand in his. The warmth of his touch felt so gentle and safe. He leaned in closer to me, and then kissed my lips. I moved into him and surprisingly felt like I wanted to kiss him back. It was a soft, warm embrace, and I knew where it was going to lead. I gently rubbed at his crotch and could feel he was hard underneath his jeans.

"This isn't a great idea, Steve. Although I do want to, of course," I whispered.

"Me too, big time. I always have." He smiled and pulled at my jumper, inching it up then over my head. With that, I stood up and slid my jeans off, letting him see me in my underwear, ready and waiting for his touch. Ready to be wanted and needed by someone else felt like the most natural thing, giving me a much-needed confidence boost.

"Wow, well, I didn't expect this, Louise," Steve acknowledged. Although I couldn't help but think he was the liar this time around. What had he thought, inviting me over and kissing me? It was such a cliche, but I couldn't seem to stop.

I sat in his lap and undid the buttons on his top to feel his muscular pecs beneath it. I undid his belt and tossed it to the side, then unbuttoned his jeans and pulled them down so I could see his manhood, hoping he was as well-endowed as Jack. To my utter surprise, he did have a large cock, and I could see that he was circumcised. I looked down at him, taking in his ripped muscles glistening in the tiny slither of sunlight streaming through a gap in the curtains. I rose up and down, riding on his hard cock, feeling every inch of him inside me. I couldn't help but appreciate his toned, smooth body—he was certainly hot, and I was enjoying having sex with him, but I just couldn't help thinking of Jack. I knew I was only sleeping with Steve to feel better about myself; to get affirmation that someone else wanted me, and, in a twisted way, to get back at Jack. Although he would never know, so what would be the point?

Steve had his eyes closed the whole time, moaning every so often and grinning with delight. Steve was handsome all right; he could have any girl he wanted, and I focused on enjoying feeling the warmth of his sexy, muscular body with him deep inside me.

"Louise, just to let you know, I'm not going to come, I find it hard to relax and fully let go," Steve professed awkwardly, like it had been an issue for him before.

"Yes, you will. I will make sure you do!" I declared, smirking as I bent over and placed his cock inside my mouth, determined to finish him off.

I couldn't say the same for myself. As much as Steve was so beautifully, aesthetically pleasing, he was just not Jack. He didn't get deep into my mind like Jack did. He didn't give me butterflies like Jack. He didn't turn me on like Jack always could.

Steve moaned and I knew he was about to come. Feeling the hot, salty semen in my mouth, I swallowed every last drop, sucking it dry, watching him squirm and groan with pleasure. Pleased with the result, knowing I could help him, I stopped and leaned back against the headboard.

"Wow, I loved that, it was brilliant! I can see why Jack always used to go on about sleeping with you so much." Steve beamed like a little child in a sweet shop. Great, so Jack shared our intimate details with his mates. *Oh, things just got better and better*, I thought to myself. "Want some pizza?"

"No, I'm OK. I had better get going. I've got an early start tomorrow." And with that I got up, got dressed, and left. I felt guilty for being with Steve, even though I wasn't Jack's girl. I knew I had crossed an invisible line. In a perverse, twisted way, I felt good. Like I had got my own back at him, but mostly I felt guilty, unfulfilled, and wished I hadn't been so easy.

I doubted whether Jack would actually care anyway. I mean, if he had wanted me, why weren't we together? Why hadn't he fought harder to stay with me?

28

A month later, I met Sean at a small bar in Covent Garden, London. It was a warm, balmy summer evening and I was out with Sarah, Nicole, and Felicity. I was decidedly drunk that night and spotted a cute guy propped up at the edge of the bar, along with a large group of his mates. I noticed that he kept looking over at me, so I smiled politely back at him, hoping he would come over.

The more I checked him out, the more attractive I found him. He was tall, muscular, casually dressed in a white Lyle & Scott T-shirt, light blue jeans, and fresh, bright white trainers. He had thick, straight, blond hair cut short. Not my usual type, although he had a defined chest—you could tell he worked out, which was something that I definitely liked. I imagined running my hands through his hair and outlining his chest with my fingertips. I let my mind wander and smiled at him every time he looked my way, hoping to strike up a conversation.

Nicole declared that she wanted to go to the toilet, and Felicity and Sarah decided to follow. I agreed to stay at the table to guard our bags and keep the table, secretly hoping that the cute guy at the bar would take the opportunity to come over to me without the watchful gaze of the other girls upon him.

I was right: within a couple of seconds, he came over to my table. "Hi, I couldn't help but notice your beautiful smile. Do you mind if I sit down here?" He gestured to the empty seat beside me.

"Go ahead, and I couldn't help noticing, my friend, that

you are indeed gorgeous," I said, trying to act as sober as I could, pointing directly in his face. "What's your name? I think I would like to take you home!" I slurred, confident that it would happen.

"Haha, well, yeh, me too. My name is Sean." He leaned his head back and laughed, beaming at me, taking my hand and pulling me closer toward him. I could tell that he wanted to kiss me, so I moved in, leaning my head toward his and he leaned in and kissed me. It was passionate and I could tell from that moment on he was going to be a lot of fun, a welcome distraction.

"Well, that was unexpected." I smiled, looking him up and down, wishing we were alone.

"You haven't told me your name yet," he replied.

"Louise. Where are you from, Sean?" I was intrigued and wanted to get to know him better, wondering what he worked as and where he lived.

Felicity came back first, eyed me, and went straight to the bar. I stopped kissing Sean and went over to her, dragging Sean along too. "Flic, meet Sean. He's lovely. I'm sure he can introduce us to all his great friends too!" I chuckled.

Felicity looked at me, rolled her eyes, and laughed. I knew she wanted to meet someone, and I still wanted to get to know Sean a little more.

The other girls soon joined us, and we all sat down back at the table, continuing to talk. Sean introduced us to his friends. The drinks were flowing, and everyone was chatting, laughing, and joking about. Sean moved closer to my side to hear better, he had told me, although really it felt like he was trying to make another move on me. I couldn't help but smile.

I looked over at Felicity and I could see she was getting on with Sean's friend Jay the most. She was easing into his personal space subtly, circling her fingers over the rim of her glass seductively.

"Alright, Flic?" I shouted, winking at her.

"Yes, Jay was just telling me about his job as a car sprayer. What a unique job!" She winked back at me.

Sean continued our conversation, asking questions about what I worked as and where I lived. He appeared straightforward, as if what you see is what you get. I liked that about him and wanted to get to know him more.

Suddenly the others decided they needed food and got up to find menus. Sean and I continued to talk. "Would you like another drink, or are you in a hurry to get to the others?"

I smiled, knowing full well there was no way I was in a rush. I was enjoying his company and outlook on life far too much.

"Yeh, go ahead, I'll have that extra drink if you don't mind?" I felt like I was on a proper date. It was nice to be given some attention and be with someone who genuinely seemed interested in what I had to say. I hadn't had that in so long, it made me feel like a young girl on her first date all over again. He was attentive and hung on my every word.

The little twinkle in his eye and his sweet smile made me want to take him home there and then. The effects of the alcohol certainly made me think of all the things we could do together. Although I could sense that he was a kind soul, I could also tell he had a certain edge about him, something that set him apart from others. He was undeniably my type, I thought to myself.

"Can I have your number?" Sean asked sweetly.

"Of course!" I replied as we swapped numbers and agreed to meet up soon. That night I went home feeling high. It was a great distraction from Jack and my past.

29

Sean invited me over to his house that Friday, a week to the day we had met, and I accepted straight away, eager to see him again. We had been chatting a lot over the phone, but nothing was like being with someone face to face, gauging how they were feeling and being able to touch them.

"Well, why don't you come over about 8 p.m., I'll get some dinner going and we can watch a film? How about that?" Sean declared on the phone. Clearly, he had already organised it in his own mind.

"Sounds perfect. I can't wait to see you again."

"Me neither! Is there anything you don't eat?"

"No, just surprise me!" I replied, eager to sample his culinary skills. For some reason he struck me as someone who knew how to cook well.

"OK, will do! Right, I'll text you the address and obviously give me a call if you get lost. See you at about 8 p.m. on Friday."

"Looking forward to it!" I replied, genuinely excited to see him again.

Friday soon came around. I had settled on my tight black faux leather trousers, a black lace blouse with a red push-up bra underneath, and black heels. *Sexy but understated*, I thought as I looked myself up and down in the mirror one last time, satisfied with the way I looked.

I got into my car, typed his address into the sat nav, and got on my way. It was only a forty-five-minute drive away, and I vaguely knew the area.

Once at his, I double-checked the address, checked my makeup in the rearview mirror, and parked the car. Hand poised to ring the doorbell, the door suddenly opened. "I saw you pull up, glad that you came. Come on in." Sean beamed eagerly at me as I stepped inside.

The flat was a new build, quite small but modern with clean lines and was tidy inside. Masculine, to say the least, as there were no ornaments or soft furnishings, but it felt comfortable all the same. I loved a good nose about; you could tell a lot about a person by their home.

"Let me take your coat. Would you like a drink? Wine, tea, coffee?" Sean was being utterly gentlemanly.

"Here, thanks," I said, passing him my coat as he hung it up next to the front door. "What wine do you have?"

"White or rosé."

"Oh, rosé please." I admired his pre-emption of such a perceived feminine drink to get for tonight.

"Coming right up," Sean declared and went into the kitchen to pour us some drinks. I took the opportunity to sit down on his comfortable, slightly greying fabric sofa and composed myself. Sean sauntered back in with two large glasses of wine. He placed one in my hand and sat down, squished up to me on the sofa as we clinked our glasses together. "To good health!"

"So, what have you decided to cook tonight then? I can't wait to see!" I opened the conversation, feeling slightly nervous suddenly.

"There is this bakery near my work that makes unbelievably good handmade pies. So, I got a couple for us to sample!" Sean smiled at me, proud as punch.

"Oh, delish!" I exclaimed. "Do you want a hand with anything?" I asked, continuing the conversation as I looked around the room, taking in his decor.

"No, I'm fine thanks. I've got it all under control. Let me put the TV on while I finish in the kitchen. I'll be back out in a moment."

I flicked through the channels and looked around, eager to go and have a nose about. I decided to ask where the toilet was.

"The door to your right," Sean shouted from the kitchen, clearly not letting me in.

"OK, fab, thanks," I replied as I slowly took a look about the flat. There was a gorgeous white wooden multi-picture frame filled with photos of various people, family I assumed, Sean amongst them. He looked gorgeous in all of them. I suddenly felt a rush of excitement that I was with him here now and hopeful for the date.

Returning to the living room, I sat down on the sofa and changed the channel again. I wasn't used to waiting around or being waited on, although it felt nice to be taken care of.

"Right, do you want a top-up?" Sean came back in and refilled my glass without waiting for an answer. I knew I had to be careful with the amount I was drinking as I had driven to his and needed to be able to drive home.

"Anyone would think you are trying to get me drunk!" I laughed as he poured the wine up to the top of the glass.

"Me? Never! Maybe just a bit more relaxed, that's all." He winked. "Dinner is ready, I will bring it out now." I stood up and moved over to the small, round glass dining table in the corner of the room and chose a seat.

"Here you are, madame." Sean smirked as he placed a beautiful dish in front of me and then his opposite. "Tuck in!"

"This looked gorgeous, thank you!" I exclaimed as I cut open the magnificent pie filled with creamy chicken and asparagus, next to a bed of salad and a huge pile of minted new potatoes.

The conversation flowed and Sean brought out a hot chocolate pudding made by Gu for each of us as we sipped our drinks and got to know each other better. He was smart, sexy, and funny, and I was waiting for him to make a move.

"Did you want another drink? Or is that your limit?"

"I'd love one, but I drove here."

"Your car is fine parked there if you wanted to leave it overnight?"

"Is that right?"

"Why don't you get a taxi home and pick it up in the morning, unless you have another idea?" Sean flirted and as he reached over to collect our plates, I grabbed his arm and beckoned for him to kiss me. He bent down and softly kissed my lips, stopping just in time to ensure I was left wanting more.

"Well, I guess I could be persuaded!" I smiled.

"Hold that thought," Sean uttered as he put the dirty dishes back into the kitchen and cleared up whilst I downed my wine for Dutch courage, hoping that this would be our moment.

"More?" Sean asked. "It's decision time—I have a couple of local taxi firms that we could use, it's no problem."

"Yes, I'd like more," I replied, hoping that he would get the hint as he poured a large glass once again and turned the lights down low.

"Here, why don't you come and sit down next to me?" Sean asked, patting the sofa that we had previously been so bashful and coy sitting together at.

"Of course!" I obliged and squished right up next to him, smiling sweetly, wondering if now was going to be the time.

He took my glass and placed it on the floor, leaning in and kissing me passionately as he ran his hand down from my neck to my breasts, cupping them and squeezing them softly. "Did you want to take this into the bedroom?" he asked, ever the gentleman.

"Do you?" I asked, unfamiliar with actually being asked, so used to being directed in situations such as this.

"Of course, but only if you are ready?" he offered.

"I'm ready!" I exclaimed and stood up, taking my drink with me as I followed Sean into his bedroom.

Sean shut the blinds and turned off the light, leaving the door open so there was a slither of light shining in from the hallway. He came over and brushed my hair from my face, looked directly into my eyes, and slowly undid my buttons one by one, checking that I was OK with the situation.

I felt uncomfortable with such attention and grabbed my drink, downing it again.

"Easy tiger, I won't bite." He laughed as he slipped my blouse off and onto the floor, staring at my breasts. I moved in closer and tugged at his belt, unlooping it and pushing his T-shirt up as he pulled it off. He then unclipped my bra, exposing my naked torso, and kissed my decolletage, edging further down to my breasts whilst I unzipped my trousers and slipped them down to the floor.

"My, my, what a beautiful body you have. Come here." Sean beckoned as he threw back the duvet on his bed.

I stood beside it and unbuttoned his jeans, tugging them down to the floor to see his erect penis through his tight white boxer shorts. I was pleasantly surprised that it was bigger than I had thought. I got into his bed and laid down. Sean followed and traced his fingers down the side of my body, tickling my hips and leaving my skin tingling. I eased my knickers down and spread my legs, hoping he would get the message. Sean obliged and dived straight in.

"Wow, you certainly know your stuff," I laughed as he licked and sucked my body.

I returned the favour and pulled his boxers down, grabbing at his cock, placing it in my mouth as he groaned with delight. Eager to have him inside me, I asked if he had any protection.

"Just in here," he said as he leaned over to his old pine bedside cabinets and pulled a condom out of the top drawer, ripping the packet open with his teeth and then sliding it down his shaft as he pushed me down and spread my legs open once again.

He placed himself inside me and rhythmically pumped in and out with his eyes closed. I grabbed at his pert bum and pushed him deeper inside me, moving with his body as he let out a loud groan. It was clear that he had come. Unfortunately for me, I was nowhere near close.

"Sorry babe, I haven't had sex for so long. You're so hot, I couldn't hold it in," he explained.

"That's OK. I loved you licking me though," I said, hinting for him to get back to it and finish me off.

"Is that so?" Sean asked as he removed the used condom and placed it in his bin. Climbing back onto the bed, he dived back in headfirst, licking and sucking, placing his fingers deep inside me.

I could feel myself about to climax as I ran my nails down his back, letting out what felt like a huge release of stress. Pleased I was finally satisfied by a man who seemed to care, I lay there and smiled.

"So, what film did you have in mind?" I laughed as Sean cuddled up close to me.

"Oh yeah, I had forgotten about that! Completely distracted," Sean laughed.

30

Our relationship developed quickly after our first date, and Sean and I moved in together after just six months in the cold, harsh winter. It was a nice welcome to have someone to come home to and keep each other warm by snuggling into one another in the evening. Sean worked in finance in London, and the commute was similar to his from my house, so he moved into mine and put his flat on the market, helping with the bills and being there whenever I needed him emotionally. He was mature, a safe haven for me; we were smitten with each other.

Jack had faded into a mere distant memory. Although, of course, from time to time he popped into my thoughts. I quickly pushed them away, knowing he was no good for me. I realised that I was in the best position I had ever been in, emotionally and financially, and I truly had stability.

Sean was a decent family type of man. He knew what he wanted and went for it wholeheartedly. There was no messing about with him. It shouldn't really have been a surprise at all when eight months after moving in together, Sean proposed to me. I was shocked but thrilled to be asked, and immediately accepted. It was a whirlwind romance, but I was enjoying the ride so far. *What's the worst that could happen?* I thought to myself.

The funny thing about life and the timing of everything is that I believe everything happens for a reason. Within a week of the proposal, I found out I was pregnant. Of course, it had happened a lot earlier than both of us had originally wanted, but similarly we were over the moon. I felt content, excited, and exactly where I should be in life for once and knew that I was going to keep the baby this time.

We decided to push the wedding forward as quickly as we could. I didn't want to be heavily pregnant walking down the aisle to Sean or looking back at photos not feeling my best. We found the most beautiful country manor house close by that did civil ceremonies and we booked it with eight weeks to go. I would have been fourteen weeks pregnant on the day, hopefully having just had our first scan and all being well. Everyone would know. I was so excited and put my all into planning the wedding down to the very last detail.

It was going to be a small affair, close family and friends only. We didn't want to spend too much, saving every extra penny we could for things for the baby, knowing that was our priority. Life was looking up, and I felt thrilled that things were changing for me.

3I

The week before the wedding, I was feeling jittery. I hoped that I had gotten everything completed and that everything was in order. There was just so much to organise, and work had been busy, although they were also understanding when I took the millionth phone call of the day regarding wedding stuff.

That Wednesday night after dinner, I placed the plates in the sink and called out to Sean.

"I'm going to pop out now and get my underwear and wedding dress, OK? I'll leave them at my parents, so there will be no peeking!"

"Sure, see you shortly, have fun," Sean answered without looking up, sipping on his cup of tea, staring at the TV.

I drove to the most exquisite wedding dress boutique located in the next town and parked in the main car park. I pressed the bell on the edge of the beautiful, polished black door to announce my arrival. Two ladies came out at once, handing me my dress and the bright white glossy satin underwear, ushering me into a cubicle to try it on one last time.

The dress was extremely tight, and I had to get both assistants to pull the fabric together to zip it up. I breathed in and looked in the mirror. It certainly looked better now they had made the alterations to it, and I felt like a princess. I was utterly pleased with my decision on the dress. I paid the money, thanked them profusely, and walked back to the car with the dress held up high on a hanger covered in a white canvas bag, hoping that it would zip up all right on the big day.

I then got ready to go on to my parents' house to drop it all off. As I was driving out of the car park, my phone beeped to alert me to a new message. I quickly looked down to see the name that flashed up, but it was just a number that wasn't stored in my phone. Instantly I recognised it as Jack's number. In disbelief, I pulled over to a safer place and opened the message. My hands were shaking with shock.

"Hey how's you? What are you up to?" was all it said.

I was furious—of all the times he could have come back into my life, of all the things he could ruin, this was not going to be one of them. I wouldn't let him. I deleted it straight away and continued to drive, turning the radio up full blast to drown my own thoughts out.

Something inside me made me coil up, and tears started to run down my face. Why did he continue to do this to me? What kind of hold did he have over me so that the slightest mention of his name made me fall to pieces? I kept replaying the message over and over in my mind, wondering what he wanted from me. Had he heard I was getting married, had he heard I was pregnant? In the end, I just couldn't help myself. I pulled over again and texted back, knowing his number by heart.

"Hey, I'm OK, feeling a little sick. How are you?"

He immediately replied, asking why I was feeling sick, but I could not bring myself to tell him it was because I was pregnant. I changed the subject and asked what he had been up to instead.

Pleasantries were relayed between us, but I knew it was of no use, so I decided to leave the conversation at that and go on to my parents' house as planned. I was determined for this to work between Sean and me. Jack couldn't come between us; I wouldn't let him. Sean had been a welcome change for me, and I had made the decision that he was all that I needed, and I would stick to that.

32

Our twelve-week dating scan went well, and I was thrilled to be able to start telling people ahead of the wedding. The baby was growing as it should and I was due at the beginning of December.

Sean drove us home, and I got back into my car to head back to work. As I was driving to the office, it dawned on me that once I had told everyone about the baby, everything would change. I would need to think about maternity leave and organise the work diary around whilst they recruited someone to cover for me.

Back in the office, although it was hard being back at work and getting into it again, I was finally thrilled to be able to tell Karen my news.

"I am so happy for you. I did have an inkling that you might have been though and that's why you were getting married so quickly. Oh, Louise, this will be the making of you!" she revealed. We sat chatting about what had happened when she had her first daughter and how things had changed over the years.

"I brought her into the office with me. She would sit in her tiny little crib under the desk, while I would nurse her occasionally. She was as good as gold when she was tiny."

"Can you imagine that happening now?" I laughed. "We would get thrown out of the office!"

"Yes, it's not the done thing at all but back then there were very few rules, and it was down to your manager's discretion.

So, if it was a small family-run business, like mine was, then so long as you completed the work, they agreed to most things. Just like smoking inside the office was permitted. You would never dream of doing that now!"

"No, you wouldn't. I couldn't think of anything worse. I bet it stank," I laughed. "Right, we had best get on, Karen, I don't want anyone thinking I'm slacking already, especially John." I expressed my concern as to what everyone would be thinking as I got up and went back into my office, ready to complete what was needed of me that day.

℔

The day of the wedding had finally arrived. I slept at home the night before, whilst Sean had gone to his best man Jay's house. So, as tradition dictates, we didn't want to see each other that morning.

I had woken up nice and early, expecting Mum and Felicity to come over and get ready with me before heading off to the wedding venue together in the hired Rolls Royce complete with a black top hat driver.

"Would you like a glass of prosecco to start the day, Louise?" Mum asked, a prosecco bottle already in her hand.

"No, I'll save my one glass for the toast. I don't want to drink this pregnancy at all really."

"Of course, good plan, dear. Felicity, you'll have one with me, won't you?"

"Too right. My best friend is about to get married and have a baby! There's so much to celebrate!" she screeched eagerly, grabbing at the glass.

"Who have you booked to do our makeup again?" Felicity questioned.

"Ann, she was the wedding venue's onsite makeup artist. I loved the trial makeup she did for me last week, so I've got her coming over shortly to do all our makeup for the day."

"Aww Louise, I can't wait. You are going to make the best mum ever. You're so thoughtful," Felicity replied just as we heard a knock at the door.

"Who's that? It can't be Ann this early, surely?" I wondered out loud and went to the front door to check.

"Wait, you can't open it. It could be Sean!" Felicity practically knocked me out of the way and moved me to the side of the room before answering the door herself.

"Panic over! It was Jay dropping this off." Felicity handed me a small box wrapped in white paper. "He said it was for you, from Sean."

"Go on, open it," Mum urged eagerly, waiting to find out what it was, standing over me ready to gawp.

"Oh, my!" I declared, taking the lid off, showcasing the undeniably beautiful, bright blue Tiffany & Co. case. I trembled as I opened the package, unravelling two gold stud knot-shaped earrings. "Wow!"

"The boy did good!"

"He certainly did," I agreed, wondering where he had gotten the time and money to get them for me. "I'll put them on now, as I am assuming he wants me to wear them today."

Ann arrived shortly after I had opened the gift. Our makeup was done to perfection, and I felt beautiful, ready to see Sean and to become his wife. Mum, Felicity, and I were thrilled with Ann's magical touch.

My tummy was continuing to grow, and I had to get them both to pull at the dress like I had when I picked the dress up just so that I could get it zipped on. I was lucky that it still fitted as my rib cage had expanded and my breasts had got larger, much to Sean's delight.

Mum was wearing a pale blue Jacques Vert sleeveless A-line dress with a matching cardigan over the top and a large white fascinator in her hair. Felicity was wearing a baby blue Coast sleeveless skater dress, hugging her in all the right places with her beautiful blonde hair down, straight, and sleek, accentuating her cheekbones.

I had opted for my hair to be placed in a delicate bun, with a few loose curls tumbling down around my face to create a feminine warmth. My dress was a beautiful, white, all-over lace floor-length dress cut in an empire style, which hid my growing tummy and skimmed nicely over my hips. My shoes were simply white satin open-toe court shoes, not too high or too flat.

I had gone for a simply beautiful feminine array of a combination of pink and white roses and carnations in my bouquet, and Felicity as my maid of honour had a smaller version to hold. Sean and Jay had a single pink rose in their buttonhole arrangement, in contrast to their dapper-looking slate grey suits and crisp white shirts. It really was the simple things that mattered and having those that we loved to spend the day with us, witnessing our vows, was the most important thing.

I looked up at the clock on the wall as it turned 1.30 p.m. I was ready at last and edged to the window, watching as the car pulled up to the house to take us to the wedding venue.

"Looks like it's now or never." I gulped.

"How are you feeling?" Mum asked, placing a manicured hand on my arm, steadying my nerves.

"I'm OK. I'll feel better when the vows are over!" I laughed nervously, knowing full well it was going to be one of the biggest moments in our lives.

"Come on then, let's go!" Felicity urged, eager to get into the plush Rolls Royce and get to the venue.

The ceremony turned out to be wonderful and all went to plan. The weather was glorious.

I was exhausted by the end of the day, and I fell asleep early while the other guests partied after us.

Sean and I woke up early the next day and read all our cards and gifts together on the bed, feeling very blessed.

33

As our twenty-one-week ultrasound scan date grew closer, I was feeling extremely nervous and apprehensive. I was just hoping that the baby was still OK and healthy. I mean, it still hadn't really sunk in that I was about to have a baby! There was so much to organise and think about.

Sean and I were eager to find out the sex of the baby and at our scan we asked the sonographer if she could see any indication of what sex it might be.

"It's a boy! If you look here, I can show you," she explained, pointing to the monitor. Sean and I looked at each other excitedly. I knew Sean had been waiting for a boy and the news was thrilling.

"I can't believe it! I'm so excited!" He beamed at me, grabbing my hand and kissing it.

"Me neither. Thank goodness everything is OK."

"All the other tests and measurements seem to be fine. Is there anything you wanted to ask me?" the sonographer offered.

"No, just the picture. That's great, thank you so much!" I replied as she wiped the gel off my stomach and I sat up to button up my jeans.

"Here, do I pay you?" Sean asked, handing some cash over to the lady for the beautiful photos of our boy. "Thanks so much for your help."

Once outside, Sean embraced me tightly and told me everything was going to be fine. He was over the moon, and we were both excited.

There was a slight chill in the air and the leaves were falling to the ground, spinning and twirling in beautiful shades of amber, yellow, and red as autumn began. Although I constantly had a niggling, almost nervous feeling inside of me, I felt safe and secure when I was with Sean. I guess it was the unknown and realising that this was it, this was my future right here and now. I guess I was scared of the commitment, scared that we were rushing things, scared that the baby would change our world. I wasn't sure what the future held, but I knew I was prepared to go and give it all I had.

"We had better head back to work now," I declared.

"Come on then, I can't wait to tell my family we're having a healthy little boy," Sean replied as he plucked his keys out of his pocket and pointed them toward the car to unlock it.

The pregnancy went by quickly and I was extremely lucky. Our beautiful boy, Aston was born at seven pounds ten, and I was smitten with him immediately. He was a wonderful, cheerful, chubby baby that settled well. I was in my element. The three of us were in a love bubble; life was easy, comfortable, and without any major pressure.

I had agreed to take the year's maternity leave off work that they offered as statutory. I was lucky enough to get paid for nine months of it, pro-rata, of course. We managed to get by with scrimping on things here and there, but there was no sign of being able to move house.

I often thought about Jack, but quickly pushed those thoughts away when I realised I was happier and more settled this way. Besides, I told myself, he had never wanted to commit to me anyway, so it made sense to move on.

34

Soon cracks began to surface between Sean and me. Life together became more difficult; it was monotonous, and we were arguing more often over ridiculous things. I knew we were nit-picking at each other, but I couldn't stop myself from shouting at him when he left the milk out of the fridge or did something equally as frustrating and absurd.

"What's this? Does it need to be here?" I could hear myself screeching loudly at him one morning as I picked up yet another pair of dirty pants from the bathroom floor.

"Oh, no it doesn't, it can go in the laundry basket," Sean replied as he vigorously brushed his teeth, clearly not detecting the anger in my voice, totally oblivious to my feelings as usual. I picked up the pants and threw them into the laundry basket, grumbling at him under my breath.

The thing was, I had decided not to go back to work after my year off on maternity leave. I couldn't bear the thought of leaving Aston with anyone else and childcare was so expensive. So, although money was tight, I managed to get a small part-time job working in a local restaurant during the evening whilst Sean looked after Aston. This meant that we didn't have to pay for childcare and Aston was mainly asleep when I was out, so I didn't feel like I was missing him. I wanted to muddle through those first few precious years with Aston, while he was a baby, and I thought I could worry about a career later on.

I was wrong, however, as I did worry about where I was in life and wondered if this was what it was all about. Without passion, fun, and new experiences. I knew I loved Sean, but was I still "in love" with him? I couldn't put my finger on it and I yearned for that spark that I had with Jack. Sean was in love with me too, I had no doubt, but surely there was more to a marriage than how we were living, more existing and making do than the life I used to lead where I could feel the energy and blood flow through my veins.

One evening, whilst out at the pub with Felicity, I opened up and let her know how I was really feeling about Sean. She always had this knack of getting things out of me without me even knowing I was unloading it.

Felicity's depth fascinated me; we had so much fun on the surface, but underneath it all she understood me; she knew how I thought, and I could rely on her, as I hoped she could me.

"So, what are you trying to tell me? You can always be honest with me," Felicity asked whilst picking the label off her bottle of Bud and placing the scrapings into the ashtray next to us.

"I don't know." I was exasperated. "I'm feeling unhappy, that's all I can tell you right now. Our relationship isn't what I thought it would be." I sighed. "I love having Aston and wouldn't change him for the world, but there's something missing. I don't know, maybe the spark has just gone." I looked down at my hands, examining my nails so I couldn't look her in the eye. The chill of the cold night air crept around my neck, and I pulled my jacket closer, wrapping it around me to keep the cold at bay. I was glad that it was already dark so Felicity couldn't scrutinise every aspect of my face for any revealing answers.

"I'm sorry to hear that."

"Argh, it just feels like I am his slave, insignificant and under-appreciated. If I'm not working, and it's the evening when Aston is asleep, there is no longer any connection between us. We hardly talk, and when we do it results in arguments most of the time. I'm utterly fed up with having to do most of the work around the house. He doesn't help or even care," I blurted out, realising I had opened the floodgates.

"My life consists of a constant barrage of wiping bums, changing nappies, to pureeing broccoli and then wiping it off the table. Then by the evening, I'm either arguing with Sean or sitting in silence next to him with some drivel on the TV that neither of us is really watching. The strange thing is, Sean must notice that things aren't right. We are just arguing all the time. There's literally no let-up right now. Oh, I don't know, I think I'm just going to wait a bit longer, see how it all pans out," I offered, matter-of-fact, as if to close the subject, embarrassed that I had divulged so much of how I was really feeling and not having an answer to it.

"It must be tough," Felicity replied, almost whispering, as if she hadn't meant to say it out loud.

"Yeh, it is. But there are worse things that can happen in life, aren't there?"

"Maybe you just need some time to yourself, to feel like the old you again. You know, do some things just for you, not Sean or Aston," Felicity offered, finishing off the last gulp of her drink and slamming the bottle down on the table. I could smell the remnants of the strong, yeasty scent of beer wafting from her bottle and motioned toward it to see if she wanted another.

"Yeh, you're right. I miss my old life. I miss spontaneity and feeling like a whole person again. Not just a housekeeper and a mother, but someone worth listening to. Someone still relevant, who matters." I sighed, feeling like I'd hit the nail on the head at last. "I don't know. We should try to organise something fun. I'll go to the bar, and we can think about what to plan to get me out of this rut," I said, getting up and heading toward the bar.

I knew I loved Aston more than anything, and I genuinely enjoyed being with him, taking him on outings and cooking him healthy, nutritious meals, or at least trying to. But I also knew that something had to change. I couldn't continue feeling how I was and maybe a break or something fun would do the trick. I looked around the bar and could see lots of couples cuddled up together, getting to know one another better and all dressed to impress. I could smell deep, rich fragrances that drenched their skin, ready to seduce their new partner, making that scent a memorable moment of its own accord.

I ordered another Bud for Felicity and a vodka, lime, and soda for myself, thinking of some kind of escape that could help change my mood. I carried the drinks back to the table and Felicity was staring up at me with a huge grin on her face.

"What is it?" I was intrigued.

"Well, how about a night away up north? We could go to a club, book a nice hotel nearby, and use their spa the next day. A get-away like we used to do. There is this fab old school night happening in Liverpool next month. Let me show you." She showed me her phone and scrolled through the web pages of a 90s-themed night in one of the big clubs in Liverpool.

"Yes!" I declared. "That sounds like just what I need. A crazy night out with a spa thrown in too. We could get the train up there, then we could relax rather than worry about traffic."

"Sounds perfect. Let me check the dates with work tomorrow, you check with Sean and your work, then we can book it!"

"Amazing! I'll look into hotels nearby. Send me the link to the club and I'll start the search. I'm in!" I screeched, excited at the prospect of a mini break away from the drudgery of my current situation. "I knew you could get some perspective on this. Thanks for your support." I smiled, genuinely grateful for her company and friendship.

Felicity clinked her bottle against my glass and replied, "Always here for you. You know I understand you and want the best for you. We can get through this blip together."

"We will," I declared, taking a huge gulp of vodka, already feeling more at ease with a big smile plastered across my face. "Anyway, enough about me. What's been going on with you lately? Tell me about that guy you met online!"

"Oh, Luke, haha. Yeh, well, where should I start?" Felicity's eyes lit up, smiling as she mentioned his name.

"Show me his picture again?" I asked, hoping that Felicity would find a decent boyfriend in Luke and not some casual fling that she seemed to encourage lately.

We oohed and aahed over his Facebook and Instagram pages, and she told me about some of the sweet things he had done and the places they had already been together. I was happy for her; she seemed at ease and comfortable. Luke sounded like a gentleman, which was a huge plus.

"So when can I meet him?" I asked eagerly.

"Oh, I don't know. When do you want to?" Felicity asked coyly.

"As soon as possible. Why don't you come over to ours one Sunday for dinner, casual but quiet enough to get to know each other, yeh?"

"It's a deal. I'll see when he's free and let you know." She smiled.

35

"Did you check the timer on the oven?" I asked Sean as I pushed the butterfly clip back into my earring, checking if my makeup looked OK in our full-length bedroom mirror.

"Yes, it's got another hour. Why do you keep asking?"

"I just want it to go well!" I shouted back.

"It will, just chill out. Besides, she will probably be onto the next bloke in a month." Sean laughed.

"That's not fair! She likes Luke, and he sounds like he's got potential," I added.

The doorbell rang, so I looked out the window to check if it was them. "They're here," I told Sean.

"Got it," he answered as he went downstairs to welcome Felicity and Luke in for Sunday dinner.

"Hey!" I could hear them greet each other as they came into the house. I swished my hair one more time, racing downstairs, eager to see them both.

"Luke, it's so good to finally meet you. Let me take your coats and go and sit down," I offered, ushering them into the sitting room.

Aston was on the sofa, blanket in hand, watching *Peppa Pig* on repeat.

"So, here's little man!" Felicity exclaimed, bending down to give Aston a big cuddle.

"Auntie Flic," Aston tried to articulate Felicity's name the best way he knew how. He was always happy to see her, and she effortlessly played the doting Auntie role, even though I knew she wasn't interested in children at all.

"Can I get you a drink? Dinner will be around an hour," I offered, eyeing Luke up and realising he was a lot taller than I had envisaged. He stood as if on ceremony, clasping his hands together with a small grin on his face, and I could tell he was nervous. His wavy brown hair, longer at the front and flicked over to the side with an extremely close shaved back, reminded me of Hugh Grant in *Four Weddings and a Funeral*. His bright blue eyes and fair skin were just the right mix of the boy next door that I knew Felicity loved.

"Let me give you a hand with the drinks, and I'll surprise you, Luke!" Felicity winked at Luke and followed me into the kitchen.

"What do you think?" Felicity asked, clearly unable to contain herself as she softly closed the kitchen door behind us.

"He's tall, isn't he?" I giggled. "Argh, Sean, go in there, keep him company." I ushered Sean out of the room so that we could chat without him listening in.

"Oh, Louise, it's so good that he's here to meet you. He's nervous though, not sure if I have built you up a bit too much, but your judgement means a lot to me."

"Oh, Flic, calm down. I'm sure he's perfect. Let's get the drinks flowing and we can all get to know him better."

"Yeh, you're right. How's things with Sean?" she asked tentatively.

"Same old, same old," I replied. "I'm glad he's agreed for us to go on our night out in Liverpool next month, though. That's exciting. We should look at booking the tickets and hotel this week."

"Awesome! Pour me some wine then, don't be stingy." She laughed as I grabbed her a wine glass and a bottle of crisp white from the fridge door.

"What would Luke want to drink?"

"Do you know what, a beer will be good."

"Fab, no problem," I replied, getting a cold one out of the fridge for both him and Sean and placing them on a large tray ready to take out.

"Right, drinks ready. Let's get to know lover boy." I smirked.

"Oi," Felicity replied, laughing as she opened the door for me.

The next hour flew past. Aston got involved and got lots of attention from Felicity. Luke was quietly observant, and Sean was the perfect host, as he always was in front of others. If only he was this attentive to me when we were alone.

"Let me check the chicken," I offered, knowing the timer was about to go off. Sean followed me into the kitchen.

"He seems nice, doesn't he?"

"Yeh, I'm happy for her. This looks like it's done. I'll serve it up, shall I?"

"Great, I'll get the cutlery sorted." Sean organised. We did work well as a team, and it was nice to have his support for things like this, but something was still niggling me.

"It's ready!" I told the guests as I peeked my head around the door and watched Aston come running along.

"Come on, little fella, let's get you fed."

"I was wondering when the grub would be ready!" Luke joked.

"Not you, Aston! Cheeky," I laughed, realising Luke was trying to be witty.

I had placed Aston at the end of the table, and Sean and I were opposite Felicity and Luke. "Cheers!" I offered my drink up for a toast. "Here's to good food and good friends!"

"Cheers." Aston held his Sippy cup up as we all laughed and tucked into the home-cooked delicious roast chicken dinner.

I couldn't help but notice how well Felicity and Luke were behaving together. They appeared the epitome of happiness. I realised I missed that feeling, the first flush of excitement and willingness to overlook any bad habits that the partner may have. A longing to be with them 24/7 and the excitement that the future held.

I turned to Sean and forced a smile. He rested his hand on my knee and smiled back. I felt nothing, complete emptiness when he touched me. I knew from that moment on that I had to get out of the relationship.

Over the next few months, I thought of Jack more often than I should have and couldn't help but want to speak with him. I wondered how he was getting on and what he had done with his life. Although I thought fondly of him, I realised he had not wanted a relationship, so I felt I did the right thing by not waiting around for him to reciprocate my feelings—or at least that's what I kept telling myself.

※

"You can't give it to him like that, you have to model it and show him how it's done. Please cut it up!" I snapped as Sean grabbed at Aston's fork, shoving a huge piece of meat onto it without cutting it. "How can you expect Aston to be able to chew or swallow it like that?" I asked.

"Why are you like this?" Sean asked as he placed the fork back down, staring me straight in the eye.

"Like what?" I asked, staring back at him, full of rage.

"You're determined to cause an argument, about anything."

"I'm not. I don't want an argument at all, but we always end up in one. I'm allowed to voice my opinion, aren't I?" I snapped, turning my back to Sean and continuing to tidy the dirty dishes away, desperate to go over and help Aston with his food but reminding myself not to interfere.

"Well then, what's the problem? I'm the one feeding him, so just let me do it," Sean stated, clearly exasperated.

Aston was looking up at Sean, wide-eyed and patiently waiting for the next mouthful.

"I'm trying to help, that's all. I want him to be able to feed himself and the best way is by showing him what to do," I continued.

"The best thing is not to argue so much in front of him."
Sean looked down at Aston, smiling and trying to create calm
once more.

"Mummy, Daddy fighting," Aston said as I turned away,
too worried that if I continued looking on, I would cry.

"Well, Mummy can't let Daddy get on with anything without interfering," Sean replied. I turned back around and scowled
at Sean—he could not stoop this low and use Aston in an argument.

"Sean, don't. Just don't," I shouted, closing the dishwasher
and then wiping the sides clean so vigorously I thought I
might tear a hole in the cloth. "I'm done." I acknowledged my
feelings. "That's it."

Pissed off, deflated, and with nothing left to give, I went
up to the bedroom and sat trawling the pages of Facebook
on my phone, looking for Jack's account. Bingo! After about
thirty minutes I found him and immediately, without thinking it through properly, requested for him to be my friend.

Settling down for a night in front of the TV, I felt a tinge
of excitement that maybe, just maybe, Jack might accept the
friend request and I could speak to him. I knew it was a long
shot, but I couldn't stop thinking about him.

The next morning, I woke up and instantly regretted
requesting him, worried that it would be a gateway to other
things. I tried to keep telling myself to stop being so foolish,
that it meant nothing and that he would most likely ignore it
anyway, so I pushed it to the back of my mind, just like I had
done with him 1,000 times before.

Lo and behold, that evening he accepted my friend request!
Intrigued as to what he was up to, I immediately went onto
his page and scanned his pictures. Shocked, I soon realised he
had moved and was now living in the USA.

In his recent photos he looked mature, happy, and peaceful, not the energetic, funny man that I once knew. I was happy
for him, and I felt proud of him for following his dreams and

doing something with his life.

Of course, this in turn made me think about my own situation even more, being stuck in the same town I had always been in, working in a meaningless job, trying to make ends meet and in a loveless marriage.

⁂

Finally, the day arrived for Felicity and me to go on an adventure, just the two of us, and leave our cares and worries behind. I was excited to spend a couple of days away from my current reality and to let my hair down.

It had taken a lot of preparation and planning, and I was nervous about leaving Aston for the first time, but I had written everything down in detail for Sean. Mum was also due over during the day on Saturday, so I knew she would help too.

The train journey from Surrey to Liverpool was long, but we gossiped with each other and read magazines. I managed to paint my nails and eat some lunch without Aston climbing all over me. In my opinion, it was utter calm and bliss—just what I needed.

"I think we're nearly here, Flic," I said as the train started slowing down, passing through more of a built-up area with office blocks and high-rise flats whizzing past.

"Woo woo!" she answered, excitedly gathering her belongings back into her overnight bag, cramming them in one by one.

Once we arrived at the impressive Liverpool Lime Street station, we quickly exited into the bright and airy platform. We hailed a cab, asking them to take us to the DoubleTree Hilton hotel, which was near Level nightclub. From looking at the reviews and pictures on their website, I was keen to try out the spa there more than anything else.

As the cab pulled up outside our hotel, I got butterflies in the pit of my stomach. I couldn't wait to get the weekend started and knew that this break would be good for my mind as well as my soul.

"You are in room 212, on floor three. The lift is behind you to the right. Enjoy your stay," the concierge informed us as we checked in. Felicity and I grabbed our bags and headed toward the lift.

"I can't wait to see what the spa is like. I think we should go there once we have unpacked!"

"Yeh, it has such great reviews," Felicity agreed.

"Here we are," I said, getting ready to step out of the lift and onto our floor. Heading down the dimly lit and narrow corridor crammed with doors on either side and a seemingly endless walkway, I held the key card to our room tightly in anticipation.

"Room 212." I smiled, turning back to see Felicity struggle to pull her case along the carpeted floor. I pushed open the door to a large, bright twin room with a floor-to-ceiling window draped in white voile, behind which I could make out the briefest outline of the city's offices and buildings.

"What do you reckon, then? Room service for drinks, or the spa?" Felicity asked, winking at me with the hotel's price list brochure in her hand and a twinkle in her eye, looking ready to dial up for some drinks.

"I can see you're ready to get the party going!" I exclaimed, laughing at her. "Go on then, just one while we unpack and get used to our surroundings. Then maybe we can check out the spa after, yeh?"

"Great, one bottle of wine then," Felicity joked.

"No, just a single vodka, lime, and soda for me, please." I smirked at her, placing my bag on the bed, ready to unload.

"OK. Oh hi, yes, room 212 here. Can I order some drinks for room service, please?" Felicity spoke into the room phone. "Great, a single vodka, lime, and soda and a bottle of Bud, please. That's great, cheers."

I took my evening outfit out of my bag and hung it up in

readiness for that night. I had decided on my faithful black tight halter-neck minidress with some black high sandals. I always felt confident in it and it was a safe bet.

Suddenly, a knock came from the door. "The drinks!" I turned to Felicity and smiled, walking toward the steady knocks.

"Thanks," I declared, taking the tray from the waiter and closing the door with my other hand.

"So, what are you wearing tonight?" I asked, handing Felicity her predictable bottle of Bud.

"I've grabbed some dark blue jeans and a sparkly V-neck top. I've even got black velvet pointy shoes, look!" She pointed to her overnight bag where one was hanging out.

"Not heels, no?" I laughed, knowing full well she wouldn't ever wear heels.

"Of course not! Who do you think I am?" She laughed, swigging her Bud back like it was the elixir of life.

I slowly sipped my vodka while admiring my friend. We were definitely chalk and cheese on the surface. She was a loud, fun tomboy with a sweet, gentle heart, and I was a girly girl with an undeniable bossiness about me. Underneath us both, there was such an unbreakable bond that bared from our need and desire for someone to truly understand and want us.

"What's the time then? Shall we get ready to go out for dinner and then onto the club, or do you think we could fit the spa in?" Felicity asked.

"It's five p.m. We could go for a wander around the hotel and then come back and get ready, yeh?" I suggested.

"Great plan," she agreed, downing her drink as I frantically tried to catch up, laughing and spitting most of it out as I did so.

The hotel wasn't anything special, just a large hotel chain that was clean and conveniently located. We took a slow walk around it, peeping in at the spa and dining rooms, finally deciding to have dinner in the hotel and take our time getting ready rather than rush to get out.

"Ready?" I asked as I blotted my lipstick on a piece of tissue so as not to stain my teeth and fixed my hair for the millionth time.

"Yep, come on then!" She grabbed her bag and linked her arm in mine, pulling me away from the mirror and snatching at my bag as she pulled me toward the door, ready for an evening of clubbing.

Level nightclub was extremely large, full to the sides with an abundance of sweaty, eager crowds, prancing about as if on parade, trying to get noticed by the opposite sex.

"The bar is over there." I pointed toward the back of the room, pushing my way through the crowds, breathing in the smell of stale sweat mixed with various strong designer perfumes. The music pumped loudly through speakers that were strategically placed throughout the club.

Looking up to my right, I could see a beautiful young girl sitting on a gigantic black metal hoop hanging from the ceiling. Dressed in black ballet flats and a bright red skimpy leotard, she was slowly swinging back and forth to gain momentum. I was intrigued to see what she would do next.

"Flic, look at her!" I exclaimed in awe.

"I know, I saw her too. You couldn't get me up there even if you paid me," she laughed, both of us staring up at the girl, watching as her movements became more rapid.

I slowly turned my head, taking in the club's atmosphere, checking out the type of people that were there, keeping one eye on the queue at the bar, eager to get a cold drink and get the night properly started.

Eventually, after getting served, Felicity and I downed the first drink with both the enthusiasm and thirst of a camel in the Sahara Desert. "Let's go over there." Felicity got up and stomped over to the dance floor, leaving me to pick up the coats.

The night went by mainly uneventfully, but we both had a great time. Felicity, as always playing the joker, danced wildly, arms and legs splayed out in some contortion whilst I looked on laughing and tried to accompany her by doing something equally as terrible and making her laugh.

The next day I woke up early with a thumping headache and a need for water by the gallon. I looked over at the twin bed near mine to see Felicity sleeping soundly.

I got up quietly and headed for the toilet. I was wide awake and couldn't just sit in bed. I was used to Aston climbing all over me, scrambling to get me up at the crack of dawn. I decided I was going to see what the spa had to offer.

"Are you coming down to the spa?" I whispered, unsure if she was still asleep. "Flic?" I gently shook her bare shoulder.

"Ugh, leave me be!" she declared.

I decided I had better go alone, so I wrote her a note stating where I was if she woke up and wanted to join me. I found a dressing gown hanging up behind the bathroom door to wrap around my body. Leaving my most respectable bikini on underneath and slipping on a pair of flip-flops, I headed down to the basement where the spa was located.

I stepped out of the hotel's tiny lift, immediately facing double doors that led into a corner room warmly lit by small Himalayan pink rock salt table lamps and low lighting, complemented by pristine whitewash walls and bright white shiny surfaces. Behind the reception desk I could see the huge indoor pool surrounded by comfy-looking grey rattan loungers.

"Hi." I smiled at the lady at the reception desk and headed toward the pool, noticing how warm and humid the room had become.

Gently laying down, fully stretching my body out on the lounger, I unravelled the huge fluffy dressing gown, revealing my bikini. Dotted along the edge of the room I could see there were beautiful round white marble and copper tables adorned with glass dispensers that were filled with cucumber water that appeared to be complimentary. I found the nearest one and reached over to pour myself a large glass. I instantly felt like a weight had been lifted off my shoulders and began to relax like I hadn't done for such a long while, soaking up the atmosphere and warmth of the heat from the pool.

Months rolled past and every time I saw a photo of Jack that popped up on social media, he was posing at some fancy venue. He was always surrounded by beautiful people and the most spectacular views. My heart would skip a beat even though I knew the pictures were not directed at me in any way, shape, or form. It made me smile to see him looking so happy, and I was genuinely excited to see where he visited next. I had no idea if he looked at my page or even if he had an interest in what I was up to, but the fact that I could escape from time to time with my thoughts of him helped me feel less alone. Although we didn't message each other, it was endearing to watch what he was up to and to feel a part of his life, as crazy as that somehow seemed.

One evening, whilst Sean was out with his friends and after putting Aston to bed, I settled down on the sofa with a cup of hot chocolate, the TV blasting out some rubbish sit-com in the background. I sat scrolling through my phone. It felt like there were pictures of happy couples in every photo I came across. They were all on these amazing holidays, and it felt like they were boasting about their joyful experiences. I felt deflated and knew I had to do something about my situation, but I was too scared to leave Sean.

I decided it was time to communicate with Jack, for entertainment if nothing else. I quickly bashed out a private message to him. *"Hey, how are things? Looks like you are having a blast over there!"*

My heart sank—oh why had I felt the need for this? It was like I was hitting the self-destruct button and he was an addiction or an escapism. I knew full well what I was doing, but it was like I was looking at it as an outsider and I could not stop myself. I kept refreshing the signal, hoping that a message would pop up from him, but it didn't. After a couple more hours of scrolling my phone and half-watching the TV, I decided to go to bed. After brushing my teeth, I crawled into bed, curling up into a ball, and fell asleep not caring that Sean wasn't even home yet.

The next morning, I woke to find Sean sprawled out like a starfish, stinking of beer next to me with his mouth wide open and in a deep sleep. I checked my phone and still nothing. I was disappointed, but at least I had tried.

I got up to get Aston out of his cot and start the day, leaving Sean to sleep off his hangover.

It was not until a week later that Jack replied, totally out of the blue in his usual fashion. *"Hey, I'm good thanks. How are things with you?"*

My heart skipped a beat seeing his name pop up in the message section, and it gave me the biggest smile. I kept rereading it, getting butterflies each time. Jack knew how to get to me; he had stolen my heart and I was utterly subservient to him. The feelings that just one little message conjured up. The wanting, the needing him, the butterflies in my tummy. He made me feel alive again!

I tried to talk myself down and kept saying to myself that it was just messaging—I was only chatting with an old friend and there was nothing in it—although I knew deep down that I wanted there to be more to this than ever before.

Over the next few months, our messages became more frequent. We got to hear about each other's new lives, and I was genuinely happy for him. It felt enough just to hear from him or to see him like one of my photos. I felt close to him that way and was satisfied that we were in each other's lives once again, albeit from a distance.

Life became harder with Sean, with more intense arguing. I ended up working in the restaurant most evenings and looking after Aston during the day. Sean and I were like ships in the night, just passing each other with no feelings involved. As he came home from work, I immediately went out. I didn't want to see him, let alone speak to him.

Time spent with Aston during the day was a great distraction and helped me focus as I was so busy with him. He settled well and was growing into a cheeky chap, always getting into things he shouldn't, and he was extremely affectionate. I could not bear to think of him without his Mummy and Daddy at his side, but I also could not bear to think of continuing the relationship the way it was. I knew something had to change, but was also scared of doing the wrong thing.

36

I started messaging Jack more often, and it was brilliant to have him there at the push of a button if I needed to chat with him. Mostly we would talk about what we had been up to that day, or if any exciting things were coming up. I knew it was completely and utterly wrong, but, as he was in a different country and we could not physically meet, I deemed it just a harmless distraction from the mundane life I was in.

One particular night when Sean was out with his work colleagues and Aston was in bed, Jack and I were messaging online. I could tell he was drunk as the messages were getting raunchier and it was clear we were both still attracted to one another in some sort of capacity, although I knew my feelings ran deeper than just sex. He was more forceful than normal and asked me for a picture of myself naked.

"Send a picture completely naked right now!" he demanded.

"Now?!" I replied, unsure of his urgency.

"Yes now, go on. Don't be shy, You've got 2 mins, go!"

I wondered if I should take a picture or not—I mean, he was being demanding but I also wanted to please him and didn't want him getting bored of me. Worried that he might have thought I had turned into a boring housewife, I decided I would see if I could get a good enough picture. So I went upstairs and tried to get into a sexy position where I could take a photo and still look desirable. Squirming around and breathing in to make myself appear slimmer, I took around fifty photos and finally I got one I was happy with. I pressed send.

"*Nice, send more,*" came his reply.

I quickly went back through the photos and found another to send, not wanting to disappoint him.

"*Send one of yourself this time,*" I invited.

Jack reciprocated by sending a close-up of his hand grasping his firm penis. I could feel myself getting more aroused.

"*I want to make myself cum right now whilst thinking of you,*" I declared.

"*Show me.*"

"*OK,*" I obliged.

I switched the video on and moved the phone closer to my jeans, resting it on the duvet so my face could not be seen. Eagerly I slid my hands down into my damp knickers and immediately placed a finger inside, playing around, getting myself extra wet and turned on.

I unzipped my trousers further and pulled my knickers down, sliding my fingers around my clit and moving the juices all around my vulva.

"*More,*" came Jack's input.

"*Hang on,*" I replied as I allowed myself to take it further and reached around to my bedside cabinet, grabbing at my vibrator, wanting to finish myself off. I imagined Jack's naked body lying by my side whilst he played with his huge, erect penis, throbbing to be inside me once again. I pushed it in further as I pictured him slowly and gently turning me onto my knees and pushing himself inside me from behind, with my legs spread open so he could go even deeper while I arched my back in delight. I let out a gasp as I wanted him inside me so much I could practically feel and remember his every move. I moaned with pleasure as I felt the walls of my vagina tighten around my vibrator as I came.

I quickly grabbed my phone and turned the camera off, pulling myself together and zipping my trousers up. Feeling like I was floating on air, wishing for him to be near me once again, wanting to feel the warmth of his kiss and his hot cum inside me, feeling like we were forever entwined.

"*Did you like it?*" I messaged.

"*Brilliant! You dirty cow!*"

"*Ha ha, just the way you like it I hope?*"

"*Of course!*"

"*Did you cum?*" I asked.

"*I did. Shame it wasn't all over you though. Maybe next time I'm back in the UK we can hook up?*"

"*Whaaat? Are you serious? Yes please! Next time you are over for sure. Just give me plenty of notice.*"

"*Well, I'm due to come back soon for my sister's wedding.*"

I couldn't believe it! Was he being serious? I would have jumped at the chance to see him.

"*I can't wait!*" I replied straight away.

"*I can't wait either,*" he replied.

I never imagined I could have met someone like him. The way he won me over, the way I felt when I was with him, the way I felt when I thought about him. No one had ever come close. He made me do things completely out of my comfort zone, pushing my boundaries, but I always felt safe. He was so open and non-judgemental. I just wished he was back in the UK with me; I wanted a chance to be with him to show him that we could be great together.

There was no way of hiding how guilty I felt, and I knew that this could not go on. I had to finish things with Sean and not string him on. I wanted to have a clean break.

37

I found it hard to escape the thoughts of Jack. The guilt was immeasurable and even in everyday occurrences he would always pop back into my thoughts. I tried to push the thoughts away, but I knew I couldn't be with Sean while my heart belonged to Jack. With or without him, it was unfair on Sean and, of course, poor Aston. I hated the thought of breaking up our family unit, but Sean deserved better—he was a good man and I had done wrong.

"Sean, please can we talk? We need to sort things through."

I told Sean I wanted to separate and that I still cared for him but that I could not be with him anymore. There was no big fanfare or any arguing between us. Sean had obviously been expecting it too, which made me sad as we had clearly stuck together for longer than we should have.

38

I had arranged to meet up with Jack when he came back to the UK for his sister's wedding. We continued messaging each other whilst Sean and I sorted through the divorce and house sale. It was agreed that I would have Aston seventy percent of the time, but that he would stay at Sean's every week at some point depending on what was going on that week. Things remained amicable between us, which I knew helped Aston deal with the breakup easier knowing that Mummy and Daddy still got along.

Eventually, the day came to meet up with Jack. I was so nervous and excited as I waited patiently in my car for Jack to turn up. It was a warm summer evening, but it was dark and I hadn't a clue where I was. I kept checking my phone for messages to say that he was on his way. I couldn't understand why he was not just phoning me. I tried to shrug these thoughts away and be positive that he was not going to let me down and that we were going to have a great night together.

Finally, he came sauntering around the corner, grinning like a Cheshire Cat. He opened my car door and gave me a kiss on the cheek. He immediately asked where we were going.

"I haven't booked anything. I didn't want to until you turned up."

"Why have you not booked anything? You've had hours to organise it!" Jack shouted at me.

Stunned, I shouted back, "I was with my friend, you could have booked something, I did not know where you were so I had no idea what was near you or if you would even turn up!"

We both sat there, frantically searching our phones, looking for a nearby hotel. The great reunion had not started off well, and I was deflated.

"Well, I might as well go home to my parents then."

"Fine, if that's what you want, I will drop you off," I answered, holding back the tears. How could he act this way? How could he be so mean, and why was he being so aggressive toward me?

After phoning around ten local hotels, we eventually found somewhere nearby that had a suite available, although at an extortionate cost. Once we were there I began to relax, taking in his gorgeous physique and wanting him to touch me. I handed my card over at the reception desk and Jack promised to pay me his half back in the morning. I smirked, guessing I would probably never see the money again. "OK, babe," I replied, trying to keep the peace.

The concierge showed us up to the room, trying to fit the key in the lock, but to no avail. He rushed off, asking us to wait there whilst he found a new one. I couldn't resist Jack any longer and kissed him passionately, unbuttoning his shirt and reaching down in his trousers to feel him already hard. I bent down to unleash it, wanting him in my mouth and to taste him.

"No, not here," Jack whispered. I jumped up and heard the concierge return. He opened the door for us and we went in.

Jack immediately sat on the bed, turning the lights low, and took his clothes off. I lifted my dress and straddled him, wanting him to touch my skin, to kiss and caress me. I leaned over and placed him in my mouth, taking every inch of him in.

"I've missed this so much. I knew you were good, but I forgot how good you actually are at this, mmm," he groaned as I continued. He moved his head down between my legs and licked me frantically, placing a finger inside me at the same time like he couldn't get enough of me. I smiled and moved his large manhood between my legs, inserting it in slightly, gauging his reaction. His eyes widened as he gave me that innocent, loving look he always did. I pushed him further in and I couldn't help but hum with pleasure, excited that we were finally one.

"You're so tight and wet, it feels incredible," Jack repeated over and over. We rocked back and forth, screaming with delight, quickly changing positions and feeling each other's bodies throughout each transition.

Suddenly he told me he was about to finish and quickly pulled himself out of me. "Swallow," he demanded. I reached down and enjoyed sucking up every last drop with extreme excitement as he squirmed.

After we cleaned ourselves up, he asked if I was OK and if I had enjoyed being with him. His tenderness showing through again made my heart skip a beat. I was happy, content, and snuggled into his chest.

"You know, you do have a wonderful body, babe."

"Hmmm, thank you, but I don't feel it's as good as it once was!" I exclaimed.

"You've had a baby, you look staggering." Jack was caring. Deep down underneath all his hard exterior, I knew he cared about me. If only I had children with him instead, I knew he would have been the man that I needed, supporting me, not taking over and arguing, not expecting me to be anything but myself. I sighed, realising that some things just couldn't be changed or forced.

We fell asleep cuddling, my head on his chest as I dreamt peacefully.

Suddenly during the night, I woke up with a start as Jack screamed in his sleep. "Sorry, I always seem to do that lately. I guess it's just too much going on in my head."

"You woke me up!" I laughed. "It's OK, try to rest," I replied, snuggling up to him once again, feeling the heat from his chest as I stroked it, trying to reassure him but his hands wandered and slowly started caressing my back, stroking me up and down. I rolled over, smiled, guiding his hand between my legs, wanting to feel him inside me once again.

"Well, I could get used to this every morning." Jack grinned at me, taking my hand and placing it over his hard, warm, erect penis.

"Good morning to you, Mr. Wyatt!" I exclaimed as I bent down and put him in my mouth. He groaned with delight as I sucked and licked him.

Jack pulled me up and bent me over onto my front, grabbing my hair and rubbing at my vagina. Then he licked his finger and plunged it deep inside me, holding my hips as he did so. Turning to look over my shoulder, I squared him up, straight in the eye. He then pulled my face around the other way and thrust himself deeper and deeper into me, pushing down on my back, ensuring that I could not move out of that position.

He took complete control and always seemed to dominate me in a way that no one else had. There was a twisted part of me that enjoyed the games he played whilst we had sex, and, knowing how much his body desired me, plus the fact that I could take it away from him at a moment's notice, made me feel in control, not him. I screamed and groaned with so much pleasure and passion that I was sure that people in the nearby rooms would be able to hear us.

"I need to be quieter, but I can't help it, babe," I panted.

"I don't care, let them hear," Jack replied, clearly getting turned on at the thought of someone listening to us. He soon pulled out and directed his cum straight onto my back. I quickly covered my head with the pillow.

"Not on my hair," I laughed, knowing that I had just washed it and had not brought my hair dryer with me to sort it out. I couldn't bear Jack to see me with "au naturelle" hair!

"Sorry, I just got carried away with you lying there next to me. I couldn't contain myself, you sexy minx."

"Well, I am glad to be of service!" I directed back at him

and got up to go to the bathroom to clean myself up. Jack rolled over and started to go back to sleep. My mind was racing. I couldn't sleep and rest any longer, so I asked if he minded if I watched the TV quietly while he slept some more.

"Go ahead, babe," Jack answered. I flicked through the channels, not really able to watch anything properly; I couldn't get a phone signal either. Looking over at him made my heart skip a beat. I truly had never felt this way about anyone before, but I hated it too. I felt deep down that he didn't want anything more from me, but I couldn't help myself with him. I was like putty in his hands, wishing he wanted me the way I wanted him.

After an hour or so Jack stirred. "Feeling fulfilled, are you now?" I whispered in his ear, stroking his chest as he snuggled into me.

"How did you guess?" he laughed, looking up at me with his beautiful, warm brown eyes. I leaned down to kiss him.

"We had better get up and get ready. It will soon be time to hand back the key," I said, getting up and heading to the shower.

Soon we were both ready to leave, and I looked about the hotel room, trying to see if we had got everything, when Jack pushed open the door and let it slam in my face as if he was in a hurry to get out. I was feeling rejected already. Trying not to let this get to me, I continued on behind him, thanking the desk staff, imagining they saw us as a couple and wondering what we must look like together. Through the car park he continued to walk quite a way out in front of me, like he did not want to be seen with me.

"Are you OK?" I asked, closing the boot with our bags inside.

"Yes, are you?" he replied, placing his hand on my shoulder.

"You seem in a hurry. Like you want to get away from me."

"Not at all. I'm sorry if you feel that way." Jack looked me in the eye as he opened the passenger door and got in.

"OK. Right, which way are we heading? I have no idea where we are now it's daylight, it all looks different."

"Let me type it into your phone so it can navigate us back. What's your pin code?" Jack asked, grabbing at my phone.

On the way home Jack was pleasant enough, asking me about my relationship with Sean, my son, and my job. It was almost as if he was interviewing me; there seemed to be no feeling behind it. He talked about how his sister was getting married the next day and that he had prepared a poem.

"Oh, read it out, go on, I'd love to hear your take on a marriage," I carefully enquired, interested to know his thoughts.

"Love is for eternity, Love is found deep within,

Love is not always easy, and love should be without sin,

Love is a verb, thinking of another's feelings, ensuring they are cared for,

Love is not simply just a feeling; it is something you know deep down to your core."

"That's a lovely poem, Jack, heartfelt! I never knew you had it in you." I nudged him and winked. "How do you feel about saying it in front of all those people? Will you be nervous?"

"Oh it's fine, it will be great." He shrugged nonchalantly, then changed the subject. "So, tell me more about your ex. Tell me what he works as. Does he earn a lot of money?"

"He is in finance. It's very dull but he does well for himself, yeh," I replied nervously, not wanting Jack to feel inferior to Sean at all.

"Great," he replied matter-of-factly.

The rest of the journey was filled with an awkward silence other than Jack giving me directions. We pulled up outside his parents' house and said our goodbyes. He kissed me on the cheek goodbye.

"I hope the wedding goes really well. Send me some pics and hopefully I can see you after it?" I asked cautiously.

"Speak to you soon, gorgeous, and drive carefully." He slammed the door then off he went, not even looking back at me.

I immediately phoned Felicity to tell her what had happened. "Wait, let me put you on speakerphone," I insisted as I unfolded the whole story all the way home.

"Do you think you will see him again?" she asked.

"No, probably not. I just don't get the feeling he is that into me. Oh, I don't know. I'd like to see him again, but I am not sure it will happen." I sighed.

Once I got home, I kept relaying what had just happened, not really believing that I'd actually spent the night with him. I couldn't help the feelings that were bubbling up inside of me; I really didn't want him to get into my head and heart like he had before. I kept thinking I should have guarded myself and not met up with him. I felt that he didn't feel the same way I did, and I had to try to forget what had happened between us, as hard as that may be.

An hour later, Sean was back to drop Aston off. I had to put it to the back of my mind and continue being the best mum I could to Aston.

Once Sean said goodbye to Aston and left, I found it increasingly hard to not think about Jack again. I just wanted to know what he was thinking and feeling, and I desperately wanted to speak to him. I had to resist. I needed a distraction.

39

That weekend Sean, Aston, and I had booked to go to Legoland in Windsor for a family day out. Sean and I still got on and we often spent time together with Aston to show union as his parents and confirm how loved he was.

Jack was still at the forefront of my mind and, remembering he was at his sister's wedding, I wondered if he was thinking of me at all. I still hadn't heard from him and knew that he was going back to America soon, so I caved in and decided to message him asking how he was. I followed it up with a picture of myself laughing in Legoland sitting by one of the rides, making the peace sign with my fingers held up.

Jack eventually replied about three hours later. *"That looks awesome, hope you're having a great time."*

"Yeh, it was great. Are you free to meet up tomorrow night?" I asked.

"I can't sorry."

"Oh, that's a shame, got a better offer have you?" I asked, knowing full well I was not his priority any longer now that he had gotten what he wanted. I felt deflated all over again.

"No not at all, I'm seeing family," he replied.

"Ah, OK. How about next Saturday night? I'm out in town with some friends, could we meet up then?"

"Sounds perfect. Can't wait to see you."

My heart skipped a beat again. I was constantly on tenterhooks. Whether he wanted to be or not, he was certainly in complete control of my emotions.

I spent the rest of the day on cloud nine, throwing myself into having as much fun with Sean and Aston as I could. Aston was exhausted by the end of the day and as I tucked him in at night, he told me how much fun he'd had.

"I loved spending time with you today too, Aston. It was lovely to go there for a treat."

"Thank you, Mummy, I loved being with you and Daddy," he replied as he closed his eyes tight and drifted off to sleep. I turned the light off and realised how lucky we were to still get along so well, and that Aston was able to be with both of us as often as we could.

Late that evening, Jack texted asking if I could meet him there and then. Why did he always do this? I couldn't just come out at the drop of a hat, even though I was desperate to see him.

"I can't, you need to give me more notice," I replied.

"Just say you have a family emergency and get a babysitter," he tried persuading me.

"I can't babe, I want to see you, believe me, but I can't get out right now. I need to plan these things."

After ten minutes of waiting for a reply, I got myself ready for bed and went to go to sleep.

I woke up to a message from him asking what I was doing and if we could sext. I felt bad that I had not seen it until the morning and texted immediately, asking if he could meet up that day. There was no reply.

A couple of hours later I messaged again, telling him that Aston was at his grandparents' house and I was free all day.

"I'm in London for a meeting today at eleven, then tomorrow I'm at Lord's Cricket ground watching my cousin play cricket there," he replied, proud as punch.

I just wanted more time with him. I knew he was planning on going back soon, but I did not want to miss the opportunity to tell him how I felt and how much I wanted to be with him and find out how he truly felt about me.

The next day I received a picture text from Jack whilst he was at Lord's. He looked gorgeous in a crisp white shirt neatly ironed and dark jeans surrounded by his family. He had a drink in his hand and looked immensely happy.

"Oh, you sexy beast, go send me something naughty," I replied. Lo and behold he went into the toilets and took a snapshot of his cock. I was in fits of giggles. The dirty bugger! I decided to return the favour and send him one of me in my underwear.

"Mmm love that, you tease."

"Certainly am babe, I want to get you turned on whilst you are out in public, it makes me laugh at the thought of you being out with a semi on and no way of relieving it."

"You dirty cow," came his reply. It was so funny, just that little bit of messaging had set me up for the day. I loved our banter and the fact that he was on my level.

Saturday night came. We had texted earlier in the day to work out where we should go, and I had explained that I was out with a friend of mine, Kiera, and her husband, Marcus.

"Don't wear knickers again. That turned me on big time," Jack had requested. Kiera and Marcus were incredibly open sexually and were often asking me to join in with them. I had been chatting to Marcus over the recent weeks about what they had got up to and had told him about Jack. I told him how I had felt and how much Jack and I were suited in the bedroom. Marcus, of course loved to hear all the gory details and kept on and on about meeting Jack and watching us have sex. I had told Marcus that it wasn't going to happen unless he paid me £1,000 for the act. Marcus agreed.

I relayed this all back to Jack, keeping him in the open, and Jack had said that he was up for it so long as he got to keep some money too. I was shocked and surprised as I wasn't even sure that I could do it. I told Jack that I was going to be out, and he arranged to meet me in town at 9 p.m.

To keep the momentum going, I texted Jack at 7 p.m., showing him what I was wearing in a video and the fact that, as requested, I had no underwear on.

"Gorgeous, such a shame I am unable to make it out tonight."

WAIT WHAT...when was he actually going to tell me he couldn't make it? I was furious.

"Why, what's happened?" I questioned.

"Family dinner. I totally forgot about it babes."

"I'm so upset."

"I'm upset too," he replied, adding a crying emoji face.

There was no apology, no care for how I had carefully planned the evening, letting myself down not to mention Kiera and Marcus too.

I carried on my night and drank myself stupid so I could not feel the pain anymore. It didn't matter where I was, at home or out—those painful feelings followed me.

I messaged him around midnight asking if I could pop over. There was no reply.

The next day went by slowly. My head was thumping, and I had a huge hangover. I hadn't heard any more from Jack and tried to push it to the back of my mind even though I was desperate to speak to him.

"Why don't you care?" I messaged, just wanting straight answers once and for all. Drifting off to sleep, I wished I hadn't met him, and wished I also had more self-control with him.

I woke with a jolt as my alarm went off. I immediately checked my phone, hoping for an answer.

"It is not that I don't care, we lead different lives, and I am here, you are there. Nothing will change. All the best."

I put my phone down and the tears began to fall like huge water balloons bursting open onto my chest in great wells. It was truly over for good this time. I had tried in vain and yet again I was not good enough. I was hurt. I was shaking, sobbing uncontrollably, my body would not stop. I was wondering how I could ever go on again without him in my life. It was as if he was my drug; he brought sunshine into my darkest days and gave me light. He inspired me to do better and be better. He accepted me for who I am. I accepted him. He was both my pleasure and my pain. He lit my life up like no other and I now felt completely dead inside. My heart was broken, my tears were flowing, I felt like there was no joy left to be had. Sitting there in the confinement of the bathroom, I must have been there for nearly an hour. Analysing what had just happened, regretting my messages pushing him to that limit like I had done so many times before. It was like a vicious cycle, year upon year. I knew I was wrong to beg, to try repeatedly, but I did not know how to stop. My heart could not take it any longer and I had to pull myself together. I could not let him control me like this for any more time than he had already done.

All I wanted was the kind of love that fulfilled my desires, a love that turns my world upside down and a love worth drowning for, worth all the pain in the world for a chance of tomorrow love that will push you to do what you have never done for anyone else and will never do again, love that you can never escape. I did not want mediocre love. Was that too much to ask for this life?

I was upset and wanted to see Jack before he flew home again, so I messaged him asking to see him, desperate to just say goodbye one last time and put closure on it, I guess.

He said he was busy but asked for a video for the road, ever so politely typing, "Show me how you fuck your toys!"

Of course, I did as was asked and sent the video I had made all those months ago but got nothing back. No reply, no nothing.

"What Jack wants, Jack gets," I sent. I was so upset. The thought of him leaving the country was debilitating and I could not stop crying.

How dare you make me feel this way. How could I be so open, so welcoming, loving, trusting, naive, foolish, raw, whilst you were so guarded and narcissistic? My heart was broken into a thousand pieces, shattered from all the times he had hurt, used, reeled me in and why had I let him knowingly each time, thinking will this be it, is this it, he won't do it again this time.

Over the next few days, I slowly took stock of how much he had controlled my life and how much time and energy I had given him throughout my day. I slowly stepped away from my phone and pushed every thought of him to the back of my mind. Eager to gain some kind of clarity.

The house took a few months to sell, and Sean and I felt like we were in limbo during that time. I found a house, smaller than the one I had before, close to Aston's school and the centre of town so I could get to work, and Sean found a house further out, bigger for the same money. We jointly took care of Aston, and I still valued Sean's parenting skills and included him as much as I could.

Sean quickly found a new girlfriend. I was hesitant about him introducing her to Aston at first, but it all turned out OK.

Months passed and the seasons changed. I watched as the sun rose and set. The weather turned cold and Christmas passed by in a daze. Slowly the nights were getting lighter and the days warmer. Jack's presence was always felt, and my heart was constantly heavy. I thought about him daily but had to keep going onwards, trusting in the universe and the plan it had for me. Trusting that I would eventually heal. Trusting that I would find the love that I craved and had experienced with him, but with reciprocation and no doubts or fears in my mind that this person genuinely loved me without the need for game playing.

Sometimes love hurts, sometimes it's joyous and it lasts. Sometimes it's a painful reminder of what is just out of reach. The main thing I guessed was not to lose hope and to stay true to yourself. What will be will be—I had to keep that faith inside myself or I would lose a grip on reality.

Would this be it? Would this be how my life played out until the day my heart beat no more? Would I pine for this love, a love that was so vibrant, so unique, so passionate and raw? Would I ever find anything like this again? Would anyone ever fulfil my heart the way that Jack had? Would I ever get over him? Would I ever find a connection that made me in awe of how I could actually feel? Would I ever feel so much joy with another human being? My heart ached to have this kind of love forever, to be near such a unique man again. He brought things out of me that I never knew existed, made me feel safe to be who I am, made me want to be a better person, a person who I should have always been, not someone who society made me feel I should be.

Beep beep went my phone... The familiar sound of a text from my phone and a message from none other than Jack...my heart skipped a beat one more time!

He was clearly drunk and was replying to an old message that I had sent asking if things were OK now. He was back in the USA. He sent lots of messages asking what I was up to and as I was still missing him, I couldn't wait to reply and get stuck into the banter. Things quickly turned dirty, and he asked me for nude photos.

"Just send it NOW, this is boring," came his replies.

"I can't, I'm cooking dinner."

"Well, I will block you then."

Dumbfounded, I put my phone down, gobsmacked that it had just happened. He was trying to control me, control my emotions. Thoroughly annoyed, I decided to leave it, knowing I could not produce a reply as to how I was feeling or even if he deserved it.

"SEND NOW."

I decided to trawl through my phone and found an older picture of myself in the mirror showing off some new underwear, bending over with a close-up. *Whoosh* went the sound of the message sending. I hoped to get one back.

"Is that it? Ha ha rubbish. Send me another or I seriously will block you."

I couldn't believe it. He was literally being abusive but on texts! What had I ever done to him? I was seriously wound up but did not respond. I decided to sleep on it and message him in the morning and ask what he was playing at.

"Sorry babe, I was so drunk and did not mean any of that."

"It was downright abusive. I did not deserve it."

"No you didn't. I am sorry. Look, let's just leave this now?"

Great, so he hadn't gotten what he wanted and decided to call it off. Gaslighting me into making it look like it was my fault for not sending him the kind of pictures he wanted! He was acting like I was being boring and that he did not want anything from me anymore. The fact that I did not feel comfortable sending him these things was neither here nor there in his mind. It was ridiculous, controlling, and downright rude. I was furious.

I got on with my life and tried to forget all about Jack. He infuriated me all the time. I just wanted him to put his guard down again, for us to be together, but there was always something that seemed to get in the way.

Common sense crept in and of course he was right; he was out there, young and carefree, living his best life while I was here, doing the same things that I had done a thousand times before. It couldn't work like this, and he obviously didn't feel the same way as I did.

40

Time went past and before I knew it another year had gone by. Felicity and I decided to go out one evening whilst Sean had Aston. We headed into town and ended up in the bar that I had first gone to with Jack when we met to talk about the pregnancy. It always brought strange memories back to me.

I looked over at the bar and saw a figure standing there that looked just like Jack! I could tell he had just gotten back from the gym. His skin looked flushed and dewy and he was pumped. All I wanted to do was kiss him, be near him, rip his clothes off, and have him inside of me. I wanted to feel the warmth of him inside me, feeling every thrust go deeper and deeper. I wanted to kiss his neck and run my hands through his hair, feeling the shape of his neck as I pulled at his bottom lip, sucking it urgently, wanting him inside me.

"Hey!" I grinned as I shimmied up to the bar and stood close to him and his friends, trying to get myself noticed.

"Hey, how are things?" Jack looked up at me.

"Great, what brings you back here? Are you visiting family?"

"No, I'm back for good," Jack replied. My heart leaped into my mouth as I almost fainted.

"Back for good?" I stammered. *Well, well, well,* I thought. This could be our time, no distractions, no nothing, just us. Pure and honest this time. Or so I hoped.

"Would you like to go over to the toilets over there and have some fun?" He gestured to the door hidden in the corner of the room. I smiled and followed him.

He kissed me immediately and pushed me against the wall. I pulled him in close and he slid my dress up to my hips, moved my knickers to the side, and placed two fingers inside of me. I screamed in ecstasy, unzipped his trousers, and grabbed at his cock, placing him inside my mouth. I could taste tiny sprays of semen as I sucked.

I did not want him to come too quickly, so I stopped and led his hands back to my knickers again. This time he frantically fingered me so forcefully I couldn't help but scream aloud, moaning with delight, in awe of how he knew my body so well. He quickly put his hand over my mouth and told me to be quiet so that no one could hear us. He then lowered his hand and grabbed at my throat whilst finger fucking me until I came. It was delicious—I could not believe he was back and what we were doing!

"You, sonny, haven't changed," I exclaimed sarcastically after I moved out of the way.

"Aren't you going to finish me off?" he asked. I bent over and sucked him dry, looking up at him as he shuddered in pleasure as I sucked at every last drop.

I let him walk out of the cubicle first, giggling as I sorted my dress and knickers out, knowing that Felicity was going to be furious at me.

41

Jack and I continued our night by drinking with our friends and mingling. I was in heaven with him there and knowing he was still interested in me. It was like a dream come true all over again.

Of course, that night we went back to his place. He was living a short drive away from mine, renting a room in a shared house, and ordered an Uber back to his. He told me he was working in IT developing websites and had been headhunted to come back to the UK and work for a renowned company based in London. It was an opportunity for his career he said he couldn't miss. I was grateful that we had bumped into each other again and hopeful that this was a fresh start for us.

The room he was staying in was typical of Jack. No soul to it, an unmade bed, empty cups and spray cans strewn about the floor.

"Would you like a drink, babe?" he asked as he unbuttoned his shirt, ready to get into bed.

"No, I just want you. Come here," I said, patting the side of the bed where I was sitting, eager to hold him.

He continued to get undressed and came over to me, reaching out his hand, cupping my face, and bending down to kiss me tenderly like he was holding onto a precious jewel. I unzipped my dress and slid it down to the floor, exposing my pastel pink push-up bra and matching knickers.

"Mmmm, stunning, but let me get those off!" Jack declared as he reached around and undid the clasp on my bra.

I then felt him gently stroking my breasts, caressing my nipples as they got hard. I could feel myself getting wetter and wetter, wanting him to introduce his fingers to my vagina. Slowly, I guided his hand down toward my navel, moaning with delight, showing him how I wanted him to touch me.

I decided I needed to be on top and rolled him over, straddling him and staring down at his muscular body, my hands on his chest, riding him slowly whilst he closed his eyes, feeling that all-too-familiar rush go over us both once again.

It was amazing to have him back. So wonderful to feel him next to me again and to have that high. It was as if he had never left my side and I was hooked all over again.

We fell asleep quickly holding onto one another just like before.

42

"Are you sure you want to do this?" I asked Felicity as we got ready for another outing. "I mean, you've been there, heard it all before, and I know you don't think that much of him."

We had planned to meet Jack and his friends out in town. Felicity was excited to see Jack's friend Brad, and I couldn't wait to spend some more time with Jack. I was worried as I knew Felicity felt Jack and I weren't good together and wanted her to be sure that this night included him.

"Babe, whatever makes you happy. I know you are never going to get him out of your system unless you give it a good go between both of you, so I'm here to get it out there. I'm supporting you but I don't always have to agree with you."

"Thanks, I owe you." I smiled as I finished my makeup with some bright pillar box red lipstick. Looking at myself in the mirror, I could see I looked nervous. "You know I love him. I always have."

"I know babe, that's why I'm here with you, OK?" Felicity placed her hand on mine in solidarity.

As soon as we walked in, I could see a group of smartly-dressed men together in the corner of the bar. Then I spotted Jack. He must have heard us come in as he turned and watched me. I felt my stomach do a somersault and tried to seductively walk up to him without falling over. I grabbed hold of Felicity's hand tightly so we could walk together as she clasped my hand back, clearly feeling my nerves too.

"Hey," I said, leaning over, planting a kiss on his cheek.

"Hey gorgeous, looking hot as always," he replied, wrapping his arms around my back and squeezing my bum.

"Thanks, I do try!" I laughed.

"What would you both like to drink?"

The night carried on smoothly and we all got along brilliantly. Even Felicity seemed smitten with Jack's friend Brad.

"Did you want to come back to mine?" Brad asked. "I'm staying at a local pub for the time being, it will be a lock in about now. Go on, it will be fun. No one wants to end the night now surely!"

"Flic, what do you reckon?" I looked at Felicity as she was wildly dancing away without a care in the world. Clearly intoxicated, I knew she would love to carry on rather than go home.

"Sure, OK. Why not!" I offered.

Jack and Brad ordered an Uber, and we all bundled into it, not ready to call it a night. The car pulled up outside a small country pub called The Bull's Head, and I asked Brad if he was sure this was allowed.

"Not legally, but the owners are friends and do it all the time."

"OK, well, if you're sure we are not going to get you into any trouble," I offered, undoing my seatbelt, ready to get out.

Brad unlocked the main front door to the pub as we followed him in. It was dimly lit but there were around ten other people in the corner of the pub, laughing and joking together.

"Hey, I've brought three mates back. We're up for more drinks. Hope that's OK?" Brad stated to no one in particular at the table.

"Come on babe, let's go have some fun." Jack winked at me and pulled me in the door. I looked around and could see that it was the kitchen. He pushed me against the worktop, kissing me urgently, moving the clothes off my shoulders as he bent down, kissing every inch of me.

"Here, sit up here." He motioned toward the shiny silver

worktop. I managed to hitch myself up and sat there waiting for him to move closer, pulling at his collar and urging him to kiss me. He pushed me back and slowly spread my legs, caressing the skin up and down, and went on to move my knickers to the side as he nuzzled his head in between, licking and sucking me.

"Er, wrong door," Felicity shouted as she walked out.

"We were just messing about. We weren't having sex," I justified, more to myself than anything.

"Louise, don't be ridiculous. I don't care either way." She laughed, closing the door.

"Jack, out of here, come on. It's not the place," I urged, pulling him by the hand and off the work surface. "We can go elsewhere."

"Your place then, yeh?"

"Let's just see how Felicity is first. I don't want to just leave her." As we returned to the bar area, I could see Felicity and Brad sitting close together in a corner of their own, kissing. Brad had one hand nestled on her thigh and the other cupping her face.

"Well, they look cosy." Jack pulled at my arm, pointing over to the corner where they were sat.

"I know. Check them out!" I laughed.

"Let's get out of here, come on, she will be fine," Jack urged, letting his hand drop and firmly squeezing at my bum.

"Let me just check," I said as I walked over. "Flic, psst," I whispered so as not to bring any more attention to them. "Flic, Jack wants to go home. Are you OK with that?"

"Yeh, fine babe. Brad, that's OK, isn't it? I can get a taxi in a bit, yeh?"

"OK, well only if you're sure?" I asked.

"She will be fine with me." Brad motioned in a military-style flick off the top of his head.

"OK, well call me if you need anything," I reiterated, ensuring that she knew I would be there if she was uncomfortable.

"Babe, come on. I'll call an Uber now," Jack urged again.

"Alright, alright. Eager beaver, what's got into you?"

"Nothing, I just want to be alone with you." He laughed as he clicked away on his phone, ordering the next available taxi.

43

"Ready? I can't wait to surprise you," Jack exclaimed with an almost childlike delirium.

"As ready as I will ever be, I guess!" I agreed as I got into the passenger seat of his car. We drove for nearly two hours and reached the harbour of Poole in Dorset.

"What are we doing here?" I asked, eager to find out my surprise.

"Just wait and see," Jack teased.

"Well, this looks heavenly! I'm in," I exclaimed as I looked around at the edge of the water, eyeing a beautiful crisp white boat shimmering and gleaming in the sunshine.

"Go on, step on, I hired it. It's ours, just for today of course!" Jack winked at me, resting his hand on my shoulder, admiring the view out to sea.

"What, and the captain? You are full of surprises, Mr. Wyatt!"

"Yes, there is also a waiter here for us for the entire day if we need him. My treat babes, you deserve this and more. I know I've not been the best boyfriend to you in the past, and I want to make it up to you."

Jack reached out his hand for me to follow and board the boat. It was incredible. I had not seen anything like it before and knew it must have taken some planning. That was not Jack's usual style, so I was intrigued as to where this was going.

He grabbed me by the hips, picked me up, and swung me around. I clutched hold of the handrail to steady myself and to stop him spinning me. He laughed and kissed my neck gently, lifting my skirt and pulling my knickers to the side, and inserted a finger deep inside me, opening me up.

"Jack, don't you think people could see us? Surely this is illegal?"

"I don't care. I want you right now."

I held onto the rail and adjusted my legs, wrapping them around the ledge to balance my body and stay in the position that Jack had put me in whilst he slid his swimming shorts down. I looked below and could see he was already swollen and solid. Smiling at me, he grabbed at my derriere and lowered me down onto the tip of his penis, just touching it, teasing, and balancing my pussy just above, ready for him to enter me with one firm thrust.

It felt hot as he pushed further and I could hear how wet I was, so I spread my legs wider, letting my vagina grip his cock whilst lowering myself down as he held tightly onto my waist.

I swung my hair back, laughing, knowing that we could be seen, but this seemed to turn me on even more—the thought that maybe someone else would enjoy this moment that we had together too.

We moved together rhythmically and slowly, keeping our bodies steady in the same position. Jack moved deeper inside me whilst he looked me straight in the eye with that cold, hard, steely look I had seen so many times over that felt like he was delving deep into my soul, taking whatever dignity I held, leaving me ready to surrender my life to him.

I took one hand and grabbed his chin, pulling it closer to mine, aggressively kissing and biting at his lips whilst ramming my pussy harder down onto his cock. He pulled at the knot on my bikini top, exposing my bare breasts to the world, kissing at my nipple and tightly squeezing my breasts with his hand.

"I'm nearly there," he declared as he took a sharp intake of breath, staring at me.

"Me too, hold on," I urged as I frantically changed pace, lowering my whole self onto him, allowing him to get deeper and further into my body like never before.

"Yes," Jack exclaimed as I felt his hot, sticky semen squirt and pulse inside of me. Panting quickly, I pressed hard against him, knowing I was about to climax too, wanting to feel at one with him at this moment.

"Argh, yes, me too." I closed my eyes, feeling that familiar rush of heat run all around my body as I hit a crescendo.

"Boy you did good." I laughed as we got ourselves back together and straightened our clothes.

"You too babe."

"I think I need to go to the bathroom," I declared, pointing to the trail of white, sticky residue already sliding down my leg. "There's a lot there today!"

"I know, it's been a while. I should have pulled out, I'm sorry."

I'm sure it will be fine, I thought to myself, hoping that I was not ovulating, trying to count back from my last period to check in my head as I cleaned myself up in the toilet, which in itself was beautiful.

"Drink? Food?" Jack asked as I walked back over to him. I could see a glorious spread of buffet food laid out.

"Yes please. What a view!" I looked out behind him as the low September sun shone down, glistening on the water whilst the boat sped along.

"So where are we going?" I asked as I popped a strawberry in my mouth from the mountainous buffet in front of us.

44

A few weeks later I knew something was up when I still hadn't come on my period. I was two weeks late, which was extremely unusual for me, so I decided to take a test after dropping Aston off at pre-school. Before the results came up, deep down I already knew the answer.

I timed three minutes and then looked down at the test. The line turned blue, and I knew my life was about to change forever. I was pregnant by Jack once again, but this time there was no way I was letting the baby go, whether he wanted to or not—I was keeping it. I was carrying a part of him, a person whom I had loved for years, whom I admired, respected, and wanted so much. There was no way I would get rid of a baby that was half his either.

I texted Jack and asked him to call me when he could. Immediately the phone rang.

"Hey, you, OK? We need to talk."

"Yeh, good. OK, fancy going for a walk during my lunch break then? I'm working from home today and could do with getting out for a bit anyway."

"Sounds like a plan. Shall I pop to yours about 12.30 p.m. yeh?"

"It's a date," he replied, hanging up. I wondered if he knew what I was going to say.

I busied myself that morning tidying and doing the washing, clearing Aston's bedroom for when he came home. Eventually it was time to go to Jack's. I made sure that my hair was done and that my makeup was looking just right. I wanted to present myself in the best possible light, but was also scared that he might run a mile at what I was about to say.

We got in Jack's car and drove to a nearby National Trust site. It was a beautiful late autumn day and the sun was shining brightly through the clouds in the sky above us.

"I'm pregnant, Jack, that's it. Please listen. There is no way I am getting rid of the baby. I'm sorry but this time you don't get to choose!" I announced, out of breath from nerves.

Jack looked dumbfounded and stepped backwards, stumbling on a log behind him. I stood, arms folded, defensive and unsure of what he was about to say.

"Even if you want nothing to do with the baby, I am keeping it. It's part of me and a part of you. I will financially support it even if you are not in its life," I blurted out, knowing full well the consequences of my actions and how harsh I sounded.

"OK, Louise, is it definitely mine?"

"How dare you!" I screamed. "Of course, you are the father. Take a DNA test if you like. It's not going to be anyone else's!"

"Sorry, I don't know why I asked. I trust you, I really do. I am just in shock. Sorry." Jack looked flushed white, as if he had seen a ghost. I knew this was not something he planned, but often when you play with fire, you get burned.

"What did you expect? It was bound to happen again sooner or later. We weren't using protection if you hadn't noticed!" I tried to reason with him as I burst into tears.

"Come here." He walked over to me and gently placed my head onto his shoulder, rubbing my back in a warm, loving manner. Immediately I knew I was doing the right thing as just his touch made me feel at peace.

"We will figure this out together." He continued to hug me while I sobbed into his shoulder.

"We had better get back. You have work and I have got to go and get Aston from pre-school, and I need to sort myself out. I can't go to meet him like this." I took myself out of his grasp and looked up at him.

"I can come with you if that helps. I hate the thought of you walking off like this, it's such a lot of take on from both our sides." Jack paused, looking down at me, holding my chin up as if he was about to kiss me. I could sense the fear in his eyes and almost felt bad. I looked away and had to remind myself that it was both of us who got into this situation; we were fully grown consensual adults knowing the consequences of our actions.

"That would be nice, if you have time," I replied.

We got into his car and sat in silence. I was feeling deflated, wanting to be by his side but knowing full well that it was a constant roller coaster with him. We were better off apart, but I could not give up our baby for anything. I was scared to be carrying his baby but happy that a part of him would always be with me. It was going to be tough, but I knew I wanted this baby, and I would not let anyone try to persuade me otherwise.

"So, when are you due?" Jack asked quietly.

"I'm not exactly sure. I'm guessing in around seven months' time, in about June, if my calculations are correct. I will have a dating scan in a month I guess."

"OK. Would you allow me to come to the scan? I want to be involved, Louise. I won't mess up this time."

My heart sank. I didn't want empty promises, but at the same time I had to try to trust him. There was no other way. "Of course, Jack. I want you to be as involved as you like."

We pulled up outside Jack's house and I got back into my car, ready to drop it back at mine so we could arrive together.

"See you in a second, yeh?" I asked, giving him the option of a get-out clause in case he had changed his mind about coming to Aston's pre-school with me.

"Yep, I'll follow you back now." He winked at me. All the charm as usual. I laughed to myself.

I swapped back into Jack's car and soon enough we pulled up outside Aston's pre-school. Jack put a protective arm around my shoulder, and I looked ahead, not wanting to see his face, not wanting to put my heart out there again in case it was crushed.

We stood outside the classroom, queuing with the other parents. I could not face talking to them, so I stood in silence with Jack by my side. Eventually the door opened, and I could see Aston's face light up when he saw me, my beautiful boy. "How was your day?" I asked as he came running up to me, bending down to give him a huge cuddle.

"It was great, Mummy. How come Jack is here?" he replied, staring at Jack.

"Jack wanted to see you today too!"

"Yeh, hey buddy, give me a high five! Looks like you've had fun today judging by the paint on your shirt there," Jack laughed, sticking his hand out in readiness for a slap of appreciation from Aston.

"I'm driving, and I'm parked right over here. You coming?"

"Yeh, cool," Aston replied.

We walked briskly to the car, and I strapped Aston in the back, safely placing him on the booster seat.

"I like this car, Mummy," Aston said.

"Yes honey, me too." I winked at Jack, knowing it was his pride and joy.

"All set?"

"Yep, let's go!" I replied.

Jack drove cautiously and I could feel the tension between us even during his gear changes. I could hear the sighs of worry fall faintly out of his mouth. I felt like he thought I had put him in the situation and that it was all too fast for him.

We pulled up outside my house. "I know you have work, but do you want to come in for a cuppa?" I asked Jack, undoing my seatbelt and grabbing my bag.

"Yes, if you don't mind," he replied.

"Of course I don't. I wouldn't have invited you otherwise!" I helped Aston out of his seat in the back.

"I'll take the booster seat back and keep it here as a spare," I advised Jack and placed it in a small plastic black garden box out of the front of the house under the living room window. I got my keys out of my bag and opened my door as Aston rushed past me, dumping his shoes on the floor and running upstairs to his bedroom.

"He's in a hurry for something," Jack laughed.

"Yes, he probably wanted to carry on with his Lego that he started this morning. He loves Lego." I smiled as I took my shoes off and walked into the kitchen to make a hot drink.

"You know, Louise, we do need to have a serious conversation about all this."

"I know that. I don't know where to start apart from to say that I am keeping the baby. You can be in its life or not. I can't force you to do anything but will respect any decision you make, as I know it's difficult for you."

"You're not forcing this, Louise. Like you said, it was bound to happen sooner or later, and I knew exactly what I was doing." He came over and placed a hand on my shoulder again, gazing at me as if he wanted to kiss me. I looked into his eyes and felt the rush of butterflies in my stomach. After all this time I couldn't believe he could still do that to me, making me complete putty in his hands. He slowly placed his hand on my chin, lifting my head upwards and my lips toward his. I kissed him softly and in return his touch was tender and loving, like never before.

"Mummy, where is Marty? I can't find him anywhere!" interrupted Aston. "Ugh, you two are kissing!" He mocked us in disgust.

"I'll help you look for it." I pulled away from Jack's embrace and quickly ushered Aston out of the room, taking his hand to lead him upstairs, knowing that Marty—the soft, cuddly teddy bear he'd had since he was born—was most likely right on the floor where he left it this morning.

"There you go, son, right here, where you left it." I ruffled his hair and laughed.

"Mummy, is Jack your boyfriend now?" Aston asked.

"We are great friends, darling, and he is comforting me at the moment."

"Why are you kissing? I don't kiss my friends like that."

"Never you mind, never you mind," I replied, annoyed at myself that I had let Aston see us before anything had been discussed properly.

Once back in the kitchen, Jack handed me an herbal tea, smiling brightly. "It's peppermint, I hope that's OK. I took the liberty of choosing for you."

"That's great, thanks. Let's go in the living room then." I ushered him out, feeling uncomfortable standing there where we had kissed less than five minutes ago.

"Louise, please, stop with this barrier you are putting up. I can sense you are feeling awkward but there is no need. We have to talk things through, and I am willing to listen," he said, patting the sofa beside him, ready for me to sit there, smiling like we were going to discuss a home insurance policy or something.

Gingerly I sat on the edge, not committing to anything, wrapping my hands around the warm mug for comfort, sniffing in the peppermint tones. I just didn't know where to start, what to say, or how he was going to react. I wanted him in my life, but I did not know how he would feel about such a huge commitment. For so long I had desperately wished and had an urge to have him close to me, and now it seemed that he wanted that too, I was feeling weary, uneasy at what lay ahead of us.

"So, let's lay the facts on the table then," Jack started. "You are due in seven months. You have a scan in one month. Can you pinpoint when it was?"

"Jack, it could have been any number of times, you know

that. Stop asking stupid questions."

"OK, OK. It's a lot to take in and digest. I am trying to get my head around it, that's all."

"So basically you need to decide if you want to be in the baby's life or not. I'm not asking you to be with me, or take on a stepdad role to Aston. I'm not asking anything of you at all. It's a decision you need to come up with. By all means come to the scans, be at the birth. I won't ever deny you access, but you can't keep coming in and out of its life like you have with me. Children need consistency and it won't be fair on the child."

"I know, Louise. I know." Jack put his head in his hands.

"Look, just sleep on it. You can't possibly have all the answers now. I don't expect you to. We can talk another day and I will let you know how I am doing and when the first scan is. OK?"

Jack nodded, biting his lip as if he was holding back tears.

I felt like we had been thrown into this situation, but the reality was we had needed a make-or-break situation. We had been coasting on and off for years and it wasn't fair to carry on like this. I got up and took our empty cups back into the kitchen.

"I think it's best you go home now," I urged.

"Right, OK. Bye, buddy, I'm off now," Jack shouted up the stairs to Aston.

"BYE," Aston screamed back at him.

"Talk to you soon," I declared as I opened the front door for Jack. "Goodbye."

"Yes, take care, babe." Jack leaned over and kissed my cheek like he had done a thousand times before, only this time it felt poignant. I shut the door behind him quickly and rested my back against the wall. Not knowing how the future would pan out, I rubbed my tummy gently.

"Don't worry, you are loved so much already," I said with a tear running down my cheek, uncertain of what the future would hold but knowing that I would love and protect the baby more than anything.

45

Jack and I had arranged to meet up that Saturday lunchtime when Aston was with Sean so we could chat openly. I heard Jack's car pull up outside at noon just as we had agreed, so I picked up my bag, phone, and keys off the sideboard and went out the door to meet him.

"I'll drive," I instructed, knowing I wanted to take control of this meeting and that driving would give me a head start. "Let's go back to The Fox by the river, yeh?" It felt poignant enough to choose the pub where we had one of our first real dates. The pub he took me to after the abortion, where things took a turn. I knew it was neutral ground and I wanted a calm, peaceful setting where we wouldn't argue and could just be.

"OK. That's fine." Jack reached over and opened the passenger door to my car with an uneasy look spread across his face.

I pulled up to the familiar, uneven, rocky car park full of potholes. The leaves on the trees were swaying in the wind, the water looking inviting and cool. I looked over to the river, trying to see if there were any swans about at this time of year.

"Look, just be upfront. What do you want?" Jack turned to face me and demanded as he fiddled to get his seatbelt off.

"You know what I want, Jack. Come on, be serious here!"

"No, Louise. Spell it out for me," Jack shouted.

"Well, if I could wave a magic wand, I would love us to be together as a family unit. I know you can't bear commitment, so I am taking that out of the equation and will have the baby whether you want it or not. All I am asking is that you either stay in the baby's life or not at all."

"Babe, slow down. I want to be in the baby's life. I couldn't bear not being a part of its life. I just don't know how to commit to a relationship with you. I am rubbish with them, it's like I get all claustrophobic or something and just need my own space."

"Yes, that's when you go off and ghost every girlfriend you have ever had because you are bored. This is your time to grow up, Jack. You can't keep acting like this forever." Jack looked wide-eyed and shocked. I was never this blunt with him. I wanted to set some boundaries before we got too far along. "It's OK. I'm happy to do this alone, but what I won't stand for is the baby not having consistency from you!" I declared, barely looking him in the eye for fear of what he would say.

"Louise, if I can give you one promise, it's that I will always be there."

"Well, it better be on a regular basis, and not just when you feel like it."

"OK. You have my word." Jack leaned over to my side of the car and tried to hug me, as if finalising the deal. I sat rigid, not allowing him to, my arms folded and hostile. I knew what I wanted and was not going to accept second-best.

"Let's go in, shall we?" I steered the conversation forward as we both got out of the car. I pressed the lock button on my key fob and straightened my dress, ready for the lunch date.

"Yep, after you." Jack motioned for me to walk first.

As I walked to the entrance of the pub from the dusty car park, I couldn't help but stare at the beautiful scenic views around me. Walking past the river, I got a rush of nostalgia for the time that we had our first date and wished that things were simpler between us. Would I have changed anything that had happened, I wondered? I know I would have been more direct with Jack, set more boundaries along with practising safer sex.

The day ultimately arrived for my first dating scan. I was feeling utterly nervous as Jack had agreed to attend, but I was so scared he wouldn't turn up and just make some excuse as to why he couldn't come. Mum had agreed to be on standby should he not come over as my Dad and her were going to watch Aston whilst I was at the hospital. "Thanks, Mum, I really appreciate it. Aston's change of clothes are in his bag if he has an accident, plus his blanket is in there if he gets tired or wants it. I'm still trying to wean him off it, but he just loves it," I conveyed matter-of-factly as I headed out the door.

"No problem, Louise. Good luck and call me if you need me."

"Will do. Bye Aston," I called out as he clambered out the back door, ready to go and play in their garden.

"Bye, Mumma," he called back.

The scan was booked for 11.45 a.m. and I was parked at the hospital ready by 11.35. I sat in my car waiting for a text from Jack before getting out. I took a couple of deep breaths to calm my nerves. I hated hospitals even in the best of times—it was the smell, and they all had an eerie feeling about them. Suddenly there was a knock on my window that made me jump. I looked up and saw Jack standing there, smiling at me.

"Hey, you scared me!" I wound the window down. "Ready to go inside, yeh?" I asked.

"Yeh, ready as I'll ever be!" He continued to smile as I pounced out of the car and quickly locked it.

As we walked down toward the main hospital entrance, Jack reached out and grabbed my hand. It felt awkward as he cupped his manly hands around mine and I looked over at him, nervous for what the next hour would bring for us both.

"It's this way, in the waiting room over here." I motioned for us to go left down the long winding corridor. Doctors passed us with clipboards and their huge white overcoats, hurrying for their next appointment.

"Here, yeh?" Jack pointed to a couple of plastic chairs all by themselves, away from the rest of the line as I checked myself in at the electronic waiting area.

"Yeh, that's great." We sat in silence, with only a faint chatter of the other couples talking excitedly in the background.

"Louise Atkinson," my name was read out over the Tanoy. I looked at Jack and we got up in unison, ready to go through to the next room.

"Hi, I'm Lucy. Louise, please lie down on the bed over there and make yourself comfortable." The ultrasound technician ushered us into the dimly lit room and pointed toward the green leather bed, which was covered in a thin layer of protective white tissue, next to the huge machine. Jack followed and sat down in the chair beside the bed as I undid the button on my jeans and moved my top up loosely so the cold gel could be applied.

Jack took my hand once again and smiled. "We're in this together, OK?"

"Thanks," I replied nervously as Lucy slathered the gel over my stomach and ran the probe up and down, clicking at certain points, measuring and calculating for a few minutes.

"OK, so baby looks healthy so far, and I have your notes here with your last period. You are measuring at approximately twelve weeks, which is what you thought, yes?" Lucy asked us.

"Yes, brilliant, so roughly when will the baby be due?" I was eager to find out.

"The estimated date of delivery is April twelfth."

I looked over at Jack and smiled. I was so relieved that everything was well. "That's great. Thanks so much."

"Did you want to get a photo? The baby is in a great position."

"Yes, I'd love one," Jack piped up eagerly, checking for change in his pocket.

"OK, great. Just tell me which one you like best, and I will print it for you now."

"I can't decide, Louise. What one do you want?"

"I like that one," I said, pointing to the clearest of them all with a great side view of the baby.

"This, yeh?" Lucy clarified. "Would you like two copies?"

"Yes please," I offered, excited. "Thanks for everything and hope to see you again at the next scan."

"Oh, is that the one where we can find out what sex it is?" Jack cautiously asked.

"It is, but we haven't discussed if we are finding that out yet or not babe."

"Yes, that's right. I hope to see you both then. Thank you for your time." Lucy gave Jack the photos and held the door open, ready for her next patient.

"Thanks." Jack beamed as he walked out, pleased as punch.

Once back at the car, Jack leaned over and kissed me good-bye. I was extremely wary of his attitude. I wanted us to be together more than anything, but I also had to guard my heart and be realistic about how he had acted in the past. "Thanks for letting me come," he offered, looking deep into my eyes.

"Babe, you are always welcome. I'm telling you straight that you can be as much a part of the baby's life as you want. I just want consistency, that's all."

"I know. I promise you things will be different from now on." Jack winked at me, placing his hand on my belly. "There is more to think about now, not just you and I, but a whole other life growing inside of you. I can't wait. I'm literally buzzing just thinking about it and can't wait to tell everyone."

"Haha, Jack, it's going to be a roller coaster of emotions, but yes. I'm excited too and we can now be open about it."

"Right, I had best get back to work before the boss fires me." Jack laughed.

"See you soon."

"I'll call you later tonight," Jack promised, handing me one of the pictures he had purchased.

"Thanks. Speak then." I waved goodbye, happy that all was well and excited to be able to share the news with my parents back at home.

195

I knew that I wasn't going to tell Aston about the baby until I had told Sean. I had no idea how he would react—disappointed, I expect, but he had his own life now and I knew that he was settled with his girlfriend, so it was also a matter of time really for them.

46

The next few months flew past in a haze, preparing for the baby. Jack was renting a room in a house a few doors down from Aston and me and was being attentive and hadn't let me down once. I knew I was still in love with him but was still holding back. I wanted to make sure that we were in the right place before living together. As much for Aston's sake as mine.

Jack and I had continued to see each other and were still sleeping together. He told me I was the only one he was having sex with, but I took that with a pinch of salt. The sex was still incredible, and I loved the way he explored my growing body. He was more sensual and gentler than he had ever been before. I was the happiest I had ever been, but was so scared of jinxing things. I was trying to take things slowly and remain in control.

I was four days overdue and had planned for Mum to be there as a backup, still not fully trusting Jack. I had pre-arranged for Sean to have Aston until I was fit and ready for him to meet the baby.

Jack was on tenterhooks and popped around as often as he could. That morning I had woken up with a few twinges and knew that it was moving in the right direction.

"Morning babe. All OK?" Jack's usual message came through.

"Yeh all normal," I replied. I didn't want to worry him until I started to assess the twinges and see if they turned into contractions.

"I think you had better tell Jack," Mum declared later that

morning. I had asked her to come over and help out whilst I timed the pains.

"OK, OK, I just don't want any false alarms and for him to be waiting around, that's all."

"Louise, when are you going to open up to him? He wants to be a part of your life and he has done everything he can to show you he means what he says." Mum looked over disapprovingly at me.

I gave in. "Alright, I'll call him now."

"Hi Jack, if you want to be at the birth, I think you had better get here soon. Sean has taken Aston already and I've said he needs to listen out for his phone for updates, as I want Aston to come along as soon as I'm ready. My key is under the doormat. Just let yourself in, OK?"

"OK, I'll be there shortly. Just let me organise work and I'll be done."

"OK, bye." I put the phone down and continued to bounce on the huge exercise ball I was sitting on, hoping that it would speed things along and that the baby would be ready to come out. I had started timing the contractions early on this morning, but they were few and far between. Although I was two days overdue, I knew that the time was coming.

The contractions were certainly getting closer together and I flicked the TV on to try to distract myself from worrying.

"You can do this, Louise. Just remember how strong and capable your body is. Would you like another drink?" Mum was fussing around, but to be honest I was grateful I wasn't alone. I could feel the contractions getting more intense.

"I'll go home the minute Jack gets here, OK? But you must promise to call me if you need anything."

"Thanks, Mum, I appreciate it."

Within ten minutes I could hear the key turn in the lock and knew that it was Jack. He had been at the house more often than not lately and, true to his word, he had stepped up. I loved having him around and Aston enjoyed his company too. I was scared to admit that things were going well, and I was excited about meeting the baby.

"Hey, Jack, is that you? We're up here," I called out to the front door.

"Yeh, coming up," he shouted back, and I heard his footsteps enter the house and the front door slam shut.

Jack came into the living room where I continued to sit, bouncing on the ball and watching the TV.

"Hey, how are you feeling?" he asked, bending down to kiss me on the cheek and nodding over at Mum.

"Excited, nervous, scared. You know, all the feelings right now," I replied, air-kissing him back.

"Want me to time the contractions again to see how far apart they are?"

"Yeh. I'm hoping they are getting closer. I'm ready to meet the baby now."

"Me too." He smiled as he pulled out his phone, ready to start the timer.

"I'm off now, you two. Good luck and call me the minute the baby is here!" Mum called out, kissing me on the forehead. "I love you."

"You too," I called back.

By the time the contractions were five minutes apart, we had my bags ready and were in the car ready to go to the hospital only a short drive away.

Once we were parked safely, Jack helped me out of the car and held my hand as we slowly walked into the hospital. Taking my notes with him, he pressed the button of the lift to take us up to the delivery rooms on floor 6.

"Why, oh why are they on the sixth floor?" I asked him as we entered the small metal cubicle.

"I know. Whose idea was that?" he declared, still holding my hand and gently rubbing my back. I could tell from his eyes that he was also scared as he pressed the button with the number 6 stamped on it.

"It's OK, babe. I'm going to be with you every step of the way. Right, it's here," he urged as the lift slowed to a stop.

We walked around to the reception desk and Jack took over as I grimaced with pain at every contraction. I knew what was to come and just wanted the baby to be out. Suddenly I could feel the urge to push.

"Jack, I'm telling you it's coming." I winced through gritted teeth as I squeezed his hand tightly.

"Louise, let's get you over to a bed so the midwife can see how dilated you are." The lady behind the desk ushered me over to a bed in the room opposite.

Within minutes she was there. I took my leggings down and allowed her to check. "Yes, you're right. Ten centimetres dilated and ready to push. The baby's head is down. Let's get you into a room of your own," she urged as she wheeled me to another room.

"Please come with me," I asked Jack.

"Of course! I'm right here with you," Jack answered as he tittered along behind the bed, following me into a room where I had already started to push.

After a few minutes I knew the baby was almost out. The midwife kept encouraging me with helpful words.

"Keep going, almost there and one more push. You can do it."

I kept squeezing Jack's hand and felt like this was happening to someone else. The pain was excruciating, but eventually I could feel the baby's head emerging.

I squeezed and pushed with all my might. Feeling a burning sensation as the last part of the baby came gushing out, I moved my head down to check that all was OK as the midwife held onto the baby, wrapping it in a towel and wiping the vernix off its body.

"Is everything OK?" I asked nervously while Jack sat down in the hard office-type chair in the corner of the sterile room.

"It's a beautiful healthy boy," the midwife called out as

she placed him on the weighing scales and did the necessary checks and passed him to me, wrapped up like a soft little cuddly bear. I held him close to me, touching his soft skin and thanking my lucky stars that he had been delivered safely and healthily as I loosened his blankets and held his skin to my skin to regulate his body temperature and form a bond. He was utterly gorgeous.

"Seven pounds, twelve ounces," she advised us. "Born at 6.36 p.m. exactly."

"A boy!" I exclaimed, knowing that Aston would be thrilled with a brother. I looked up at Jack and smiled. "Baby Carter it is, then! Would you like a hold now?"

"Would I ever!" he answered enthusiastically, like a child in a sweet shop excited to get their next sugar fix.

"Come over here then. I'll pass him to you. Support his head, though!" I offered while the other midwife prepared me so that I could pass the placenta.

"Would you like the syntocinon injection to deliver it?" she asked.

"Yes, that will help," I answered as I placed the baby into Jack's arms. He immediately went back to sitting in the chair, staring intently at the baby's features with a huge smile that lit up his whole face.

"Louise, if you can give me a big push when I say we can get this placenta out nice and safely."

"OK, sure." I gripped the side of the bed, knowing that more pain was to follow but that soon it would all be over.

Immediately after I had been checked over and cleaned up, I looked at Jack, who was a blubbering mess, holding onto baby Carter. "Louise, you have been amazing. Thank you for giving me this gift of life. Look at him, he's amazing. I feel so blessed. I'm in awe of you and love you so much." Jack got up and leaned over me, kissing me lovingly on my forehead and placing Carter back into my arms.

"I'll leave you two to it. Would you like me to get you

some hot toast and a cup of tea, dear?" the midwife asked.

"Oh yes, please," I agreed, knowing that my body would need re-fuelling for the next few hours ahead with trying to breastfeed Carter.

Although I loved hearing how open and vulnerable Jack was being toward me, I felt extremely uncomfortable with what he was saying. It was the first time I had heard Jack say he loved me. I wasn't sure if it was the rush of endorphins from the baby's birth or if he really meant it. Either way, I felt an overwhelming rush of love for our baby. I just wanted to protect and nurture him like I had with Aston, so I decided I was going to focus on that.

"What have I actually been waiting for? This, this is everything I have ever wanted. Louise, I want to be with you." Jack wiped a tear from his eye and placed his hand over mine.

"Jack, you are all I've ever wanted. We've both been so stupid in the past, but I'm scared. Please don't hurt me. I want to be with you too, but I need to be sure you are in it for real this time."

"I am. I want to be with you, Aston, and Carter. We can make this work. I promise!" Jack declared.

The midwife came back and handed me some much-needed toast and a hot cup of tea whilst Jack cradled Carter and I tried to rest.

47

Carter and I were discharged from hospital fairly quickly, and I was feeling well within myself. I was in love with my newborn, and I couldn't wait for Aston to meet his baby brother. I had arranged for my parents to bring Aston over to mine so that when I got home with Jack and Carter, they would be there.

"I'm so happy, Louise." Jack placed his hand upon mine as we drove home from the hospital. He looked at me, beaming from ear to ear.

I loved hearing him speak to me like that, but I was still so wary of his actions and afraid he would leave at any moment. I was trying to guard my heart, but I wanted it all more than anything.

"Me too," I replied, squeezing his hand.

We pulled up to the driveway and I could see through the living room windows that it was adorned with bright blue foil balloons and bunches of flowers. I was excited to see Aston and let my parents meet Carter.

"This is it," I exclaimed to Jack, knowing that this was the start of something special. I unclipped my seatbelt and climbed out of the car, eager to check on Carter and bring him inside.

"Welcome home!" I could hear the chants coming from behind me at the front door. Turning around, I saw Aston running up to me, giving me the biggest cuddle.

"Mummy!" he exclaimed, reaching up and nestling his head into my tummy.

"Aston," I squealed, picking him up and spinning him around, holding onto him as tightly as I could. "Would you like to meet your baby brother?" I asked tentatively.

"Yes, where?"

I opened the back door and reached in, taking Carter and his car seat out, proudly showing him off. Jack immediately came around my side and placed an arm around Aston's shoulder. "Alright buddy, we missed you."

"Look Mummy, he's sleeping!" Aston exclaimed as we all laughed.

"Come here, let me take him." Jack took Carter in the car seat inside as Mum came out to give me another welcome hug.

"Well done darling, he's beautiful. Now let's get you inside for some rest, shall we? Your Dad and I have made some lunch for us all. Let's get your strength back up too."

"Thanks, Mum, I feel so lucky. It's been a whirlwind."

"That it has." She laughed, taking my bags from the boot of the car.

That evening, after our visitors had left and I had put Aston to bed, I sat down next to Jack, staring at him as he cradled a sleepy Carter. I felt like my heart could burst. I never knew love could feel so right, so warm and enveloping this way. It was all I wanted from the start, I knew it.

Jack looked at me, smiled, leaned over, and cupped my chin, moving my lips upwards and toward his. I couldn't help but melt into him and kiss him back like my life depended upon it. It would be for keeps this time, it had to be—I would do anything to make sure it would be.

48

Jack opened the gate and placed the carrier containing the puppy on the patio. I called for Aston to come outside and meet our newest addition to the family, a little white fluffy cockapoo named Teddy.

"What!" Aston called back, peering out of the back door.

"Come here, I have someone here to meet you," I answered.

"A puppy!" Aston exclaimed, running toward the carrier, eager to get him out.

Teddy settled in well and was a calm but timid puppy. The first twenty-four hours were a blur, whizzing past in a matter of excitement, trepidation, and nervousness. Jack had said he felt like he couldn't eat because of nerves and that it was like having a newborn baby again. He was a patient, calm, loving dog and all that we could have ever hoped for.

A few months later, I was sitting in the garden, sipping on my morning tea. The sky was clear, and the sun shone down on the garden so brightly I had to squint to see into the distance. I felt content and calm. I looked around and I could not believe what we had together. I loved my boys, Aston and Carter; I was so happy just being at our new home with them.

I loved the life we had created together. Jack truly was my soul mate. We understood each other like no one else, and I knew that we were going to be together forever. Even though we had had a slightly toxic and rocky start, it was now pure magic. No one—not one other person in my lifetime—made me feel the way he did. I was utterly in love and happy with where I was in my life. I had good friends and family I could count on, two beautiful sons, and Jack was the ultimate icing on the cake.

Jack threw a tennis ball down the garden for Teddy to fetch. He then sat down on the empty wicker chair next to me. The sunshine continued to beat down on us and the sky was a clear shade of bright blue. Jack sipped the last of his tea as Teddy ran up and down the lawn, wagging his tail and chasing the bright yellow ball to bring back to us to continue the game.

"Right, it's time for me to go and earn some money, babe," Jack declared, gripping the edge of the chair as he said so. "Aston, buddy, I'm going to work now, have a great day at school!" Jack got up from the chair and shouted toward Aston. He leaned down, kissing me goodbye as he gently placed his hand over Carter's head, ruffling his fluffy morning hair.

I sat smiling peacefully, taking in the serene view in front of me. Jack looked strikingly handsome in his suit; I was still utterly in love. I inhaled each breath with pure gratitude, filling my lungs with unadulterated happiness. Knowing that this was all I had ever wanted, having it here in front of me was still a lot to take in.

I wanted to remember this moment and the feelings that it conjured forever. Life certainly has been an adventure and, as they say, "it isn't over until it's over."

About Atmosphere Press

Founded in 2015, Atmosphere Press was built on the principles of Honesty, Transparency, Professionalism, Kindness, and Making Your Book Awesome. As an ethical and author-friendly hybrid press, we stay true to that founding mission today.

If you're a reader, enter our giveaway for a free book here:

SCAN TO ENTER
BOOK GIVEAWAY

If you're a writer, submit your manuscript for consideration here:

SCAN TO SUBMIT
MANUSCRIPT

And always feel free to visit Atmosphere Press and our authors online at atmospherepress.com. See you there soon!

About the Author

EMILY MARTIN was born in the colourful 1980s and raised in the heart of Surrey, UK. She is proud to still live there along with her husband, raising their own children and Labrador dog.

Emily's love of story writing was ignited at a young age, as she often sat at an old-fashioned typewriter, conjuring up dramatic stories to add to her made-up newspaper for the family to read. After completing an extensive writing course as an adult, she had more confidence to start writing her own novels.